Four Arthurian Romances
-Eric Et Enide-

Four Arthurian Romances
-Eric Et Enide-
by Chretien DeTroys

©2011 SMK Books

Wilder Publications, LLC.
PO Box 3005
Radford VA 24143-3005

ISBN 10: 1-61720-585-0
ISBN 13: 978-1-61720-585-9

Erec Et Enide

The rustic's proverb says that many a thing is despised that is worth much more than is supposed. Therefore he does well who makes the most of whatever intelligence he may possess. For he who neglects this concern may likely omit to say something which would subsequently give great pleasure. So Chretien de Troyes maintains that one ought always to study and strive to speak well and teach the right; and he derives from a story of adventure a pleasing argument whereby it may be proved and known that he is not wise who does not make liberal use of his knowledge so long as God may give him grace. The story is about Erec the son of Lac—a story which those who earn a living by telling stories are accustomed to mutilate and spoil in the presence of kings and counts. And now I shall begin the tale which will be remembered so long as Christendom endures. This is Chretien's boast.

One Easter Day in the Springtime, King Arthur held court in his town of Cardigan. Never was there seen so rich a court; for many a good knight was there, hardy, bold, and brave, and rich ladies and damsels, gentle and fair daughters of kings. But before the court was disbanded, the King told his knights that he wished to hunt the White Stag, in order to observe worthily the ancient custom. When my lord Gawain heard this, he was sore displeased, and said: "Sire, you will derive neither thanks nor goodwill from this hunt. We all know long since what this custom of the White Stag is: whoever can kill the White Stag must forsooth kiss the fairest maiden of your court, come what may. But of this there might come great ill, for there are here five hundred damsels of high birth, gentle and prudent daughters of kings, and there is none of them but has a bold and valiant knight for her lover who would be ready to contend, whether fight or wrong, that she who is his lady is the fairest and gentlest of them all." The King replies: "That I know well; yet will I not desist on that account; for a king's word ought never to be gainsaid. To-morrow morning we shall all gaily go to hunt the White Stag in the forest of adventure. And very delightful this hunt will be."

And so the affair is arranged for the next morning at daybreak. The morrow, as soon as it is day, the King gets up and dresses, and dons a short jacket for his forest ride. He commands the knights to be aroused and the horses to be made ready. Already they are ahorse, and off they go, with bows and arrows. After them the Queen mounts her horse, taking a damsel with her. A maid she was, the daughter of a king, and she rode a white palfrey. After them there swiftly followed a knight, named Erec, who belonged to the

Round Table, and had great fame at the court. Of all the knights that ever were there, never one received such praise; and he was so fair that nowhere in the world need one seek a fairer knight than he. He was very fair, brave, and courteous, though not yet twenty-five years old. Never was there a man of his age of greater knighthood. And what shall I say of his virtues? Mounted on his horse, and clad in an ermine mantle, he came galloping down the road, wearing a coat of splendid flowered silk which was made at Constantinople. He had put on hose of brocade, well made and cut, and when his golden spurs were well attached, he sat securely in his stirrups. He carried no arm with him but his sword. As he galloped along, at the corner of a street he came up with the Queen, and said: "My lady, if it please you, I should gladly accompany you along this road, having come for no other purpose than to bear you company." And the Queen thanks him: "Fair friend, I like your company well, in truth; for better I could not have."

Then they ride along at full speed until they come into the forest, where the party who had gone before them had already started the stag. Some wind the horns and others shout; the hounds plunge ahead after the stag, running, attacking, and baying; the bowmen shoot amain. And before them all rode the King on a Spanish hunter.

Queen Guinevere was in the wood listening for the dogs; beside her were Erec and the damsel, who was very courteous and fair. But those who had pursued the stag were so far from them that, however intently they might listen to catch the sound of horn or baying of hound, they no longer could hear either horse, huntsman, or hound. So all three of them drew rein in a clearing beside the road. They had been there but a short time when they saw an armed knight along on his steed, with shield slung about his neck, and his lance in hand. The Queen espied him from a distance By his right side rode a damsel of noble bearing, and before them, on a hack, came a dwarf carrying in his hand a knotted scourge. When Queen Guinevere saw the comely and graceful knight, she desired to know who he and his damsel were. So she bid her damsel go quickly and speak to him.

"Damsel," says the Queen, "go and bid yonder knight come to me and bring his damsel with him." The maiden goes on amble straight toward the knight. But the spiteful dwarf sallies forth to meet her with his scourge in hand, crying: "Halt, maiden, what do you want here? You shall advance no farther." "Dwarf," says she, "let me pass. I wish to speak with yonder knight; for the Queen sends me hither." The dwarf, who was rude and mean, took his stand in the middle of the road, and said: "You have no business here. Go back. It is not meet that you should speak to so excellent a knight." The damsel advanced and tried to pass him by force, holding the dwarf in slight esteem when she saw that he was so small. Then the dwarf raised his whip, when he saw her coming toward him and tried to strike her in the face. She raised her arm to protect herself, but he lifted his hand again and struck her all unprotected on her bare hand: and so hard did he strike her on the back of her hand that it turned all black and blue. When the maiden could do nothing else, in spite of herself she must needs return. So weeping she turned back. The tears came to her eyes and ran down her cheeks. When the Queen sees her damsel wounded, she is sorely grieved and angered and knows not what to do. "Ah, Erec, fair friend," she says, "I am in great sorrow for my damsel whom that dwarf has wounded. The knight must be discourteous indeed, to allow such a monster to strike so beautiful a creature. Erec, fair friend, do you go to the knight and bid him come to me without delay. I wish to know him and his lady." Erec starts off thither, giving spurs to his steed, and rides straight toward the knight. The ignoble dwarf sees him coming and goes to meet him. "Vassal," says he, "stand back! For I know not what business you have here. I advise you to withdraw." "Avaunt," says Erec, "provoking dwarf! Thou art vile and troublesome. Let me pass." "You shall not." "That will I." "You shall not." Erec thrusts the dwarf aside. The dwarf had no equal for villainy: he gave him a great blow with his lash right on the neck, so that Erec's neck and face are scarred with the blow of the scourge; from top to bottom appear the lines which the thongs have raised on him. He knew well that he could not have the satisfaction of striking the dwarf; for he saw that the knight was armed, arrogant, and of evil intent, and he was afraid that he would soon kill him, should he strike the dwarf in his presence. Rashness is not bravery. So Erec acted wisely in retreating without more ado. "My lady," he says, "now matters stand worse; for the rascally dwarf has so wounded me that he has badly cut my face. I did not dare to strike or touch him; but none ought to reproach me, for I was completely unarmed. I mistrusted the armed knight, who, being an ugly fellow and violent, would take it as no jest, and would soon kill me in his pride. But this much I will promise you; that if I can, I shall yet avenge my disgrace, or increase it. But my arms are too far away to avail me in this time of need; for at Cardigan did I leave them this morning when I came away. And if I should go to fetch them there, peradventure I should never again find the knight who is riding off apace. So I must follow him at once, far or near, until I find some arms to hire or borrow. If I find some one who will lend me arms, the knight will quickly find me ready for battle. And you may be sure without fail that we two shall fight until he defeat me, or I him. And if possible, I shall be back by the third day, when you will see me home again either joyous or sad, I know not which. Lady, I cannot delay longer, for I must follow after the knight. I go. To God

I commend you." And the Queen in like manner more than five hundred rimes commends him to God, that he may defend him from harm.

Erec leaves the Queen and ceases not to pursue the knight. The Queen remains in the wood, where now the King had come up with the Stag. The King himself outstripped the others at the death. Thus they killed and took the White Stag, and all returned, carrying the Stag, till they came again to Cardigan. After supper, when the knights were all in high spirits throughout the hall, the King, as the custom was, because he had taken the Stag, said that he would bestow the kiss and thus observe the custom of the Stag. Throughout the court a great murmur is heard: each one vows and swears to his neighbour that it shall not be done without the protest of sword or ashen lance. Each one gallantly desires to contend that his lady is the fairest in the hall. Their conversation bodes no good, and when my lord Gawain heard it, you must know that it was not to his liking. Thus he addressed the King: "Sire," he says, "your knights here are greatly aroused, and all their talk is of this kiss. They say that it shall never be bestowed without disturbance and a fight." And the King wisely replied to him: "Fair nephew Gawain, give me counsel now, sparing my honour and my dignity, for I have no mind for any disturbance."

To the council came a great part of the best knights of the court. King Yder arrived, who was the first to be summoned, and after him King Cadoalant, who was very wise and bold. Kay and Girflet came too, and King Amauguin was there, and a great number of other knights were there with them. The discussion was in process when the Queen arrived and told them of the adventure which she had met in the forest, of the armed knight whom she saw, and of the malicious little dwarf who had struck her damsel on the bare hand with his whip, and who struck Erec, too, in the same way an ugly blow on the face; but that Erec followed the knight to obtain vengeance, or increase his shame, and how he said that if possible he would be back by the third day. "Sire," says the Queen to the King, "listen to me a moment. If these knights approve what I say, postpone this kiss until the third day, when Erec will be back." There is none who does not agree with her, and the King himself approves her words.

Erec steadily follows the knight who was armed and the dwarf who had struck him until they come to a well placed town, strong and fine . They enter straight through the gate. Within the town there was great joy of knights and ladies, of whom there were many and fair. Some were feeding in the streets their sparrow-hawks and moulting falcons; others were giving an airing to their tercels, their mewed birds, and young yellow hawks; others play at dice or other game of chance, some at chess, and some at backgammon. The grooms in front of the stables are rubbing down and currying the horses. The ladies are bedecking themselves in their boudoirs. As soon as they see the knight coming, whom they recognised with his dwarf and damsel, they go out three by three to meet him. The knight they all greet and salute, but they give no heed to Erec, for they did not know him. Erec follows close upon the knight through the town, until he saw him lodged. Then, very joyful, he passed on a little farther until he saw reclining upon some steps a vavasor well on in years. He was a comely man, with white locks, debonair, pleasing, and frank. There he was seated all alone, seeming to be engaged in thought. Erec took him for an honest man who would at once give him lodging. When he turned through the gate into the yard, the vavasor ran to meet him, and saluted him before Erec had said a word. "Fair sir," says he, "be welcome. If you will deign to lodge with me, here is my house all ready for you." Erec replies: "Thank you! For no other purpose have I come; I need a lodging place this night."

Erec dismounts from his horse, which the host himself leads away by the bridle, and does great honour to his guest. The vavasor summons his wife and his beautiful daughter, who were busy in a work-room—doing I know not what. The lady came out with her daughter, who was dressed in a soft white under-robe with wide skirts hanging loose in folds. Over it she wore a white linen garment, which completed her attire. And this garment was so old that it was full of holes down the sides. Poor, indeed, was her garb without, but within her body was fair.

The maid was charming, in sooth, for Nature had used all her skill in forming her. Nature herself had marvelled more than five hundred times how upon this one occasion she had succeeded in creating such a perfect thing. Never again could she so strive successfully to reproduce her pattern. Nature bears witness concerning her that never was so fair a creature seen in all the world. In truth I say that never did Iseut the Fair have such radiant golden tresses that she could be compared with this maiden. The complexion of her forehead and face was clearer and more delicate than the lily. But with wondrous art her face with all its delicate pallor was suffused with a fresh crimson which Nature had bestowed upon her. Her eyes were so bright that they seemed like two stars. God never formed better nose, mouth, and eyes. What shall I say of her beauty? In sooth, she was made to be looked at; for in her one could have seen himself as in a mirror. So she came forth from the work-room: and when she saw the knight whom she had never seen before, she drew back a little, because she did not know him, and in her modesty she blushed. Erec, for his part, was amazed when he beheld such beauty in her, and the vavasor said to her: "Fair daughter dear, take this horse and lead him to the stable along with my own horses. See that he lack for nothing: take off his saddle and bridle, give him oats and hay, look after him and curry him, that he may be in good condition."

The maiden takes the horse, unlaces his breast-strap, and takes off his bridle and saddle. Now the horse is in good hands, for she takes excellent care of him. She throws a halter over his head, rubs him down, curries him, and makes him comfortable. Then she ties him to the manger and puts plenty of fresh sweet hay and oats before him. Then she went back to her father, who said to her: "Fair daughter dear, take now this gentleman by the hand and show him all honour. Take him by the hand upstairs." The maiden did not delay (for in her there was no lack of courtesy) and led him by the hand upstairs. The lady had gone before and prepared the house. She had laid embroidered cushions and spreads upon the couches, where they all three sat down Erec with his host beside him, and the maiden opposite. Before them, the fire burns brightly. The vavasor had only one man-servant, and no maid for chamber or kitchen work. This one man was busy in the kitchen preparing meat and birds for supper. A skilful cook was he, who knew how to prepare meal in boiling water and birds on the spit. When he had the meal prepared in accordance with the orders which had been given him, he brought them water for washing in two basins. The table was soon set, cloths, bread, and wine set out, and they sat down to supper. They had their fill of all they needed. When they had finished and when the table was cleared, Erec thus addressed his host, the master of the house: "Tell me, fair host." he asked, "why your daughter, who is so passing fair and clever, is so poorly and unsuitably attired." "Fair friend," the vavasor replies, "many a man is harmed by poverty, and even so am I. I grieve to see her so poorly clad, and yet I cannot help it, for I have been so long involved in war that I have lost or mortgaged or sold all my land. And yet she would be well enough dressed if I allowed her to accept everything that people wish to give her. The lord of this castle himself would have dressed her in becoming fashion and would have done her every manner of favour, for she is his niece and he is a count. And there is no nobleman in this region, however rich and powerful, who would not willingly have taken her to wife had I given my consent. But I am waiting yet for some better occasion, when God shall bestow still greater honour upon her, when fortune shall bring hither some king or count who shall lead her away, for there is under Heaven no king or count who would be ashamed of my daughter, who is so wondrous fair that her match cannot be found. Fair, indeed, she is; but yet greater far than her beauty, is her intelligence. God never created any one so discreet and of such open heart. When I have my daughter beside me, I don't care a marble about all the rest of the world. She is my delight and my pastime, she is my joy and comfort, my wealth and my treasure, and I love nothing so much as her own precious self."

When Erec had listened to all that his host told him, he asked him to inform him whence came all the chivalry that was quartered in the town. For there was no street or house so poor and small but it was full of knights and ladies and squires. And the vavasor said to him: "Fair friend, these are the nobles of the country round; all, both young and old, have come to a fete which is to be held in this town tomorrow; therefore the houses are so full. When they shall all have gathered, there will be a great stir to-morrow; for in the presence of all the people there will be set upon a silver perch a spar-row-hawk of five or six moultings—the best you can imagine. Whoever wishes to gain the hawk must have a mistress who is fair, prudent, and courteous. And if there be a knight so bold as to wish to defend the worth and the name of the fairest in his eyes, he will cause his mistress to step forward and lift the hawk from the perch, if no one dares to interpose. This is the custom they are observing, and for this each year they gather here." There-upon Erec speaks and asks him: "Fair host, may it not displease you, but tell me, if you know, who is a certain knight bearing arms of azure and gold, who passed by here not long ago, having close beside him a courtly damsel, preceded by a hump-backed dwarf." To him the host then made reply: "That is he who will win the hawk without any opposition from the other knights. I don't believe that any one will offer opposition; this time there will be no blows or wounds. For two years already he has won it without being challenged; and if he wins it again this year, he will have gained permanent possession of it. Every succeeding year he may keep it without contest or challenge." Quickly Erec makes reply: "I do not like that knight. Upon my word, had I some arms I should challenge him for the hawk. Fair host, I beg you as a boon to advise me how I may be equipped with arms whether old or new, poor or rich, it matters not." And he replies to him generously: "It were a pity for you to feel concern on that score! I have good fine arms which I shall be glad to lend you. In the house I have a triple-woven hauberk, which was selected from among five hundred. And I have some fine valuable greaves, polished, handsome, and light in weight. The helmet is bright and handsome, and the shield fresh and new. Horse, sword, and lance all I will lend you, of course; so let no more be said." "Thank you kindly, fair gentle host! But I wish for no better sword that this one which I have brought with me, nor for any other horse than my own, for I can get along well enough with him. If you will lend me the rest, I shall esteem it a great favour. But there is one more boon I wish to ask of you, for which I shall make just return if God grant that I come off from the battle with honour." And frankly he replies to him: "Ask confidently for what you want, whatever it be, for nothing of mine shall lack you." Then Erec said that he wished to defend the hawk on behalf of his daughter; for surely there will be no damsel who is one hundredth part as beautiful as she. And if he takes her with him, he will have good and just reason to maintain and to prove that she is entitled to carry away the hawk. Then he added: "Sire, you know not what guest you have sheltered here, nor do you know my estate and kin. I am the son of a rich and puissant king: my father's name is King Lac, and the Bretons call me Erec. I belong to King Arthur's court, and have been with him now three years. I know not if any report of my father or of me has ever reached this land. But I promise you and vow that if you will fit me out with arms, and will give me your daughter to-morrow when I strive for the hawk, I will take her to my country, if God grant me the victory, and I will give her a crown to wear, and she shall be queen of three cities." "Ah, fair sir! Is it true that you are Erec, the son of Lac?" "That is who I am, indeed" quoth he. Then the host was greatly delighted and said: "We have indeed heard of you in this country. Now I think all the more of you, for you are very valiant and brave. Nothing now shall you be refused by me. At your request I give you my fair daughter." Then taking her by the hand, he says: "Here, I give her to you." Erec received her joyfully, and now has all he desired. Now they are all happy there: the father is greatly delighted, and the mother weeps for joy. The maiden sat quiet; but she was very happy and glad that she was betrothed to him, because he was valiant and courteous: and she knew that he would some day be king, and she should receive honour and be crowned rich queen.

They had sat up very late that night. But now the beds were prepared with white sheets and soft pillows, and when the conversation flagged they all went to bed in happy frame. Erec slept little that night, and the next morn, at crack of dawn, he and his host rose early. They both go to pray at church, and hear a hermit chant the Mass of the Holy Spirit, not forgetting to make an offering. When they had heard Mass both kneel before the altar and then return to the house. Erec was eager for the battle; so he asks for arms, and they are given to him. The maiden herself puts on his arms (though she casts no spell or charm), laces on his iron greaves, and makes them fast with thong of deer-hide. She puts on his hauberk with its strong meshes, and laces on his ventail. The gleaming helmet she sets upon his head, and thus arms him well from tip to toe. At his side she fastens his sword, and then orders his horse to be brought, which is done. Up he jumped clear of the ground. The damsel then brings the shield and the strong lance: she hands him the shield, and he takes it and hangs it about his neck by the strap. She places the lance in his hand, and when he had grasped it by the butt-end, he thus addressed the gentle vavasor: "Fair sire," quoth he, "if you please, make your daughter ready now; for I wish to escort her to the sparrow-hawk in accordance with our agreement." The vavasor then without delay had saddled a bay palfrey. There can nothing be said of the harness because of the dire poverty with which the vavasor was afflicted. Saddle and bridle were put on, and up the maiden mounted all free and in light attire, without waiting to be urged. Erec wished to delay no longer; so off he starts with the host's daughter by his side, followed by the gentleman and his lady.

Erec rides with lance erect and with the comely damsel by his side. All the people, great and small, gaze at them with wondering eyes as they pass through the streets. And thus they question each other: "Who is yonder knight? He must be doughty and brave, indeed, to act as escort for this fair maid. His efforts will be well employed in proving that this damsel is the fairest of them all." One man to another says: "In very truth, she ought to have the sparrow-hawk." Some praised the maid, while many said: "God! who can this knight be, with the fair damsel by his side?" "I know not." "Nor I." Thus spake each one. "But his gleaming helmet becomes him well, and the hauberk, and shield, and his sharp steel sword. He sits well upon his steed and has the bearing of a valiant vassal, well-shapen in arm, in limb and foot." While all thus stand and gaze at them, they for their part made no delay to take their stand by the sparrow-hawk, where to one side they awaited the knight. And now behold! they see him come, attended by his dwarf and his damsel. He had heard the report, that a knight had come who wished to obtain the sparrow-hawk, but he did not believe there could be in the world a knight so bold as to dare to fight with him. He would quickly defeat him and lay him low. All the people knew him well, and all welcome him and escort him in a noisy crowd: knights, squires, ladies, and damsels make haste to run after him. Leading them all the knight rides proudly on, with his damsel and his dwarf at his side, and he makes his way quickly to the sparrow-hawk. But all about there was such a press of the rough and vulgar crowd that it was impossible to touch the hawk or to come near where it was. Then the Count arrived on the scene, and threatened the populace with a switch which he held in his hand. The crowd drew back, and the knight advanced and said quietly to his lady: "My lady, this bird, which is so perfectly moulted and so fair, should be yours as your just portion; for you are wondrous fair and full of charm. Yours it shall surely be so long as I live. Step forward, my dear, and lift the hawk from the perch." The damsel was on the point of stretching forth her hand when Erec hastened to challenge her, little heeding the other's arrogance. "Damsel," he cries, "stand back! Go dally with some other bird, for to this one you have no right. In spite of all, I say this hawk shall never be yours. For a better one than you claims it—aye, much more fair and more courteous." The other knight is very wroth; but Erec does not mind him, and bids his own maiden step forward. "Fair one." he cries, "come forth. Lift the bird from the perch, for it is right that you should have it. Damsel, come forth! For I will make boast to defend it if any one is so bold as to intervene. For no woman excels you in beauty or worth, in grace or honour any more than the moon outshines the sun." The other could suffer it no longer, when he hears him so manfully offer himself to do battle. "Vassal," he cries, "who art thou who dost thus dispute with me the hawk?" Erec boldly answers him: "A knight I am from another land. This hawk I have come to obtain; for it is right, I say it in spite of all, that this damsel of mine should have it." "Away!" cries the other, "it shall never be. Madness has brought thee here. If thou dost wish to have the hawk, thou shalt pay fight dearly for it." "Pay, vassal; and how?" "Thou must fight with me, if thou dost not resign it to me." "You talk madness," cries Erec; "for me these are idle threats; for little enough do I fear you." "Then I defy thee here and now. The battle is inevitable." Erec replies: "God help me now; for never did I wish for aught so much." Now soon you will hear the noise of battle.

The large place was cleared, with the people gathered all around. They draw off from each other the space of an acre, then drive their horses together; they reach for each other with the tips of their lances, and strike each other so hard that the shields are pierced and broken; the lances split and crack; the saddle-bows are knocked to bits behind. They must needs lose their stirrups, so that they both fall to the ground, and the horses run off across the field. Though smitten with the lances, they are quickly on their feet again, and draw their swords from the scabbards. With great fierceness they attack each other, and exchange great sword blows, so that the helmets are crushed and made to ring. Fierce is the clash of the swords, as they rain great blows upon neck and shoulders. For this is no mere sport: they break whatever they touch, cutting the shields and shattering the hauberks. The swords are red with crimson blood. Long the battle lasts; but they fight so lustily that they become weary and listless. Both the damsels are in tears, and each knight sees his lady weep and raise her hands to God and pray that He may give the honours of the battle to the one who strives for her. "Ha! vassal," quoth the knight to Erec, "let us withdraw and rest a little; for too weak are these blows we deal. We must deal better blows than these; for now it draws near evening. It is shameful and highly discreditable that this battle should last so long. See yonder that gentle maid who weeps for thee and calls on God. Full sweetly she prays for thee, as does also mine for me. Surely we should do our best with our blades of steel for the sake of our lady-loves." Erec replies: "You have spoken well." Then they take a little rest, Erec looking toward his lady as she softly prays for him. While he sat and looked on her, great strength was recruited within him. Her love and beauty inspired him with great boldness. He remembered the Queen, to whom he pledged his word that he would avenge the insult done him, or would make it greater yet. "Ah! wretch," says he, "why do I wait? I have not yet taken vengeance for the injury which this vassal permitted when his dwarf struck me in the wood." His anger is revived within him as he summons the knight: "Vassal," quoth he, "I call you to battle anew. Too long we have rested; let us now renew our strife." And he replies: "That is no hardship to me." Whereupon, they again fall upon each other. They were both expert fencers. At his first lunge the knight would have wounded Erec had he not skilfully parried. Even so, he smote him so hard over the shield beside his temple that he struck a piece from his helmet. Closely shaving his white coif, the sword descends, cleaving the shield through to the buckle, and cutting more than a span from the side of his hauberk. Then he must have been well stunned, as the cold steel penetrated to the flesh on his thigh. May God protect him now! If the blow had not glanced off, it would have cut right through his body. But Erec is in no wise dismayed: he pays him back what is owing him, and. attacking him boldly, smites him upon the shoulder so violently a blow that the shield cannot withstand it, nor is the hauberk of any use to prevent the sword from penetrating to the bone. He made the crimson blood flow down to his waist-band. Both of the vassals are hard fighters: they fight with honours even, for one cannot gain from the other a single foot of ground. Their hauberks are so torn and their shields so hacked, that there is actually not enough of them left to serve as a protection. So they fight all exposed. Each one loses a deal of blood, and both grow weak. He strikes Erec and Erec strikes him. Erec deals him such a tremendous blow upon the helmet that he quite stuns him. Then he lets him have it again and again, giving him three blows in quick succession, which entirely split the helmet and cut the coif beneath it. The sword even reaches the skull and cuts a bone of his head, but without penetrating the brain. He stumbles and totters, and while he staggers,

Erec pushes him over, so that he falls upon his right side. Erec grabs him by the helmet and forcibly drags it from his head, and unlaces the ventail, so that his head and face are completely exposed. When Erec thinks of the insult done him by the dwarf in the wood, he would have cut off his head, had he not cried for mercy. "Ah! vassal," says he, "thou hast defeated me. Mercy now, and do not kill me, after having overcome me and taken me prisoner: that would never bring thee praise or glory. If thou shouldst touch me more, thou wouldst do great villainy. Take here my sword; I yield it thee." Erec, however, does not take it, but says in reply: "I am within an ace of killing thee." "Ah! gentle knight, mercy! For what crime, indeed, or for what wrong shouldst thou hate me with mortal hatred? I never saw thee before that I am aware, and never have I been engaged in doing thee any shame or wrong." Erec replies: "Indeed you have." "Ah, sire, tell me when! For I never saw you, that I can remember, and if I have done you any wrong, I place myself at your mercy." Then Erec said: "Vassal, I am he who was in the forest yesterday with Queen Guinevere, when thou didst allow thy ill-bred dwarf to strike my lady's damsel. It is disgraceful to strike a woman. And afterwards he struck me, taking me for some common fellow. Thou wast guilty of too great insolence when thou sawest such an outrage and didst complacently permit such a monster of a lout to strike the damsel and myself. For such a crime I may well hate thee; for thou hast committed a grave offence. Thou shalt now constitute thyself my prisoner, and without delay go straight to my lady whom thou wilt surely find at Cardigan, if thither thou takest thy way. Thou wilt reach there this very night, for it is not seven leagues from here, I think. Thou shalt hand over to her thyself, thy damsel, and thy dwarf, to do as she may dictate; and tell her that I send her word that to-morrow I shall come contented, bringing with me a damsel so fair and wise and fine that in all the world she has not her match. So much thou mayst tell her truthfully. And now I wish to know thy name." Then he must needs say in spite of himself: "Sire, my name is Yder, son of Nut. This morning I had not thought that any single man by force of arms could conquer me. Now I have found by experience a man who is better than I. You are a very valiant knight, and I pledge you my faith here and now that I will go without delay and put myself in the Queen's hands. But tell me without reserve what your name may be. Who shall I say it is that sends me? For I am ready to start." And he replies: "My name I will tell thee without disguise: it is Erec. Go, and tell her that it is I who have sent thee to her." "Now I'll go, and I promise you that I will put my dwarf, my damsel, and myself altogether at her disposal (you need have no fear), and I will give her news of you and of your damsel." Then Erec received his plighted word, and the Count and all the people round about the ladies and the gentlemen were present at the agreement. Some were joyous, and some downcast; some were sorry, and others glad. The most rejoiced for the sake of the damsel with the white raiment, the daughter of the poor vavasor she of the gentle and open heart; but his damsel and those who were devoted to him were sorry for Yder.

Yder, compelled to execute his promise, did not wish to tarry longer, but mounted his steed at once. But why should I make a long story? Taking his dwarf and his damsel, they traversed the woods and the plain, going on straight until they came to Cardigan. In the bower outside the great hall, Gawain and Kay the seneschal and a great number of other lords were gathered. The seneschal was the first to espy those approaching, and said to my lord Gawain: "Sire, my heart divines that the vassal who yonder comes is he of whom the Queen spoke as having yesterday done her such an insult. If I am not mistaken, there are three in the party, for I see the dwarf and the damsel." "That is so," says my lord Gawain; "it is surely a damsel and a dwarf who are coming straight toward us with the knight. The knight himself is fully armed, but his shield is not whole. If the Queen should see him, she would know him. Hello, seneschal, go call her now!" So he went straightway and found her in one of the apartments. "My lady," says he, "do you remember the dwarf who yesterday angered you by wounding your damsel?" "Yes, I remember him right well. Seneschal, have you any news of him? Why have you mentioned him?" "Lady, because I have seen a knight-errant armed coming upon a grey horse, and if my eyes have not deceived me, I saw a damsel with him; and it seems to me that with him comes the dwarf, who still holds the scourge from which Erec received his lashing." Then the Queen rose quickly and said: "Let us go quickly, seneschal, to see if it is the vassal. If it is he, you may be sure that I shall tell you so, as soon as I see him." And Kay said: "I will show him to you. Come up into the bower where your knights are assembled. It was from there we saw him coming, and my lord Gawain himself awaits you there. My lady, let us hasten thither, for here we have too long delayed." Then the Queen bestirred herself, and coming to the windows she took her stand by my lord Gawain, and straightway recognised the knight. "Ha! my lords," she cries, "it is he. He has been through great danger. He has been in a battle. I do not know whether Erec has avenged his grief, or whether this knight has defeated Erec. But there is many a dent upon his shield, and his hauberk is covered with blood, so that it is rather red than white." "In sooth, my lady," quoth my lord Gawain, "I am very sure that you are quite right. His hauberk is covered with blood, and pounded and beaten, showing plainly that he has been in a fight. We can easily see that the battle has been hot. Now we shall soon hear from him news that will give us joy or gloom: whether Erec sends him to you here as a prisoner at your discretion, or whether he comes in pride of heart to boast before us arrogantly that he has defeated or killed Erec. No other news can he bring, I think." The Queen says: "I am of the same opinion." And all the others say: "It may well be so."

Meanwhile Yder enters the castle gate, bringing them news. They all came down from the bower, and went to meet him. Yder came up to the royal terrace and there dismounted from his horse. And Gawain took the damsel and helped her down from her palfrey; the dwarf, for his part, dismounted too. There were more than one hundred knights standing there, and when the three newcomers had all dismounted they were led into the King's presence. As soon as Yder saw the Queen, he bowed low and first saluted her, then the King and his knights, and said: "Lady, I am sent here as your prisoner by a gentleman, a valiant and noble knight, whose face yesterday my dwarf made smart with his knotted scourge. He has overcome me at arms and defeated me. Lady, the dwarf I bring you here: he has come to surrender to you at discretion. I bring you myself, my damsel, and my dwarf to do with us as you please." The Queen keeps her peace no longer, but asks him for news of Erec: "Tell me," she says, "if you please, do you know when Erec will arrive?" "To-morrow, lady, and with him a damsel he will bring, the fairest of all I ever knew." When he had delivered his message, the Queen, who was kind and sensible, said to him courteously: "Friend, since thou hast thrown thyself upon my mercy, thy confinement shall be less harsh; for I have no desire to seek thy harm. But tell me now, so help thee God, what is thy name?" And he replies: "Lady, my name is Yder, son of Nut." And they knew that he told the truth. Then the Queen arose, and going before the King, said: "Sire, did you hear? You have done well to wait for Erec, the valiant knight. I gave you good advice yesterday, when I counselled you to await his return. This proves that it is wise to take advice." The King replies: "That is no lie; rather is it perfectly true that he who takes advice is no fool. Happily we followed your advice yesterday. But if you care anything for me, release this knight from his durance, provided he consent to join henceforth my household and court; and if he does not consent, let him suffer the consequence." When the King had thus spoken, the Queen straightway released the knight; but it was on this condition, that he should remain in the future at the court. He did not have to be urged before he gave his consent to stay. Now he was of the court and household to which he had not before belonged. Then valets were at hand to run and relieve him of his arms.

Now we must revert to Erec, whom we left in the field where the battle had taken place. Even Tristan, when he slew fierce Morhot on Saint Samson's isle , awakened no such jubilee as they celebrated here over Erec. Great and small, thin and stout—all make much of him and praise his knighthood. There is not a knight but cries: "Lord what a vassal! Under Heaven there is not his like!" They follow him to his lodgings, praising him and talking much. Even the Count himself embraces him, who above the rest was glad, and said: "Sire, if you please, you ought by right to lodge in my house, since you are the son of King Lac. If you would accept of my hospitality you would do me a great honour, for I regard you as my liege. Fair sire, may it please you, I beg you to lodge with me." Erec answers: "May it not displease you, but I shall not desert my host to-night, who has done me much honour in giving me his daughter. What say you, sir? Is it not a fair and precious gift?" "Yes, sire," the Count replies; "the gift, in truth, is fine and good. The maid herself is fair and clever, and besides is of very noble birth. You must know that her mother is my sister. Surely, I am glad at heart that you should deign to take my niece. Once more I beg you to lodge with me this night." Erec replies: "Ask me no more. I will not do it." Then the Count saw that further insistence was useless, and said: "Sire, as it please you! We may as well say no more about it; but I and my knights will all be with you to-night to cheer you and bear you company." When Erec heard that, he thanked him, and returned to his host's dwelling, with the Count attending him. Ladies and knights were gathered there, and the vavasor was glad at heart. As soon as Erec arrived, more than a score of squires ran quickly to remove his arms. Any one who was present in that house could have witnessed a happy scene. Erec went first and took his seat; then all the others in order sit down upon the couches, the cushions, and benches. At Erec's side the Count sat down, and the damsel with her radiant face, who was feeding the much disputed hawk upon her wrist with a plover's wing. Great honour and joy and prestige had she gained that day, and she was very glad at heart both for the bird and for her lord. She could not have been happier, and showed it plainly, making no secret of her joy. All could see how gay she was, and throughout the house there was great rejoicing for the happiness of the maid they loved.

Erec thus addressed the vavasor: "Fair host, fair friend, fair sire! You have done me great honour, and richly shall it be repaid you. To-morrow I shall take away your daughter with me to the King's court, where I wish to take her as my wife; and if you will tarry here a little, I shall send betimes to fetch you. I shall have you escorted into the country which is my father's now, but which later will be mine. It is far from here—by no means near. There I shall give you two towns, very splendid, rich, and fine. You shall be lord of Roadan, which was built in the time of Adam, and of another town close by, which is no less valuable. The people call it Montrevel, and my father owns no better town. And before the third day has passed, I shall send you plenty of gold and silver, of dappled and grey furs, and precious silken stuffs wherewith to adorn yourself and your wife my dear lady. To-morrow at dawn I wish to take your daughter to court, dressed and arrayed as she is at present. I wish my lady, the Queen, to dress her in her best dress of satin and scarlet cloth."

There was a maiden near at hand, very honourable, prudent, and virtuous. She was seated on a bench beside the maid with the white shift, and was her own cousin the niece of my lord the Count. When she heard how Erec intended to take her cousin in such very poor array to the Queen's court, she spoke about it to the Count. "Sire," she says, "it would be a shame to you more than to any one else if this knight should take your niece away with him in such sad array." And the Count made answer: "Gentle niece, do you give her the best of your dresses." But Erec heard the conversation, and said: "By no means, my lord. For be assured that nothing in the world would tempt me to let her have another robe until the Queen shall herself bestow it upon her." When the damsel heard this, she replied: "Alas! fair sire, since you insist upon leading off my cousin thus dressed in a white shift and chemise, and since you are determined that she shall have none of my dresses, a different gift I wish to make her. I have three good palfreys, as good as any of king or count, one sorrel, one dappled, and the other black with white forefeet. Upon my word, if you had a hundred to pick from, you would not find a better one than the dappled mount. The birds in the air do not fly more swiftly than the palfrey; and he is not too lively, but just suits a lady. A child can ride him, for he is neither skittish nor balky, nor does he bite nor kick nor become unmanageable. Any one who is looking for something better does not know what he wants. And his pace is so easy and gentle that a body is more comfortable and easy on his back than in a boat." Then said Erec: "My dear, I have no objection to her accepting this gift; indeed, I am pleased with the offer, and do not wish her to refuse it." Then the damsel calls one of her trusty servants, and says to him: "Go, friend, saddle my dappled palfrey, and lead him here at once." And he carries out her command: he puts on saddle and bridle and strives to make him appear well. Then he jumps on the maned palfrey, which is now ready for inspection. When Erec saw the animal, he did not spare his praise, for he could see that he was very fine and gentle. So he bade a servant lead him back and hitch him in the stable beside his own horse. Then they all separated, after an evening agreeably spent. The Count goes off to his own dwelling, and leaves Erec with the vavasor, saying that he will bear him company in the morning when he leaves. All that night they slept well. In the morning, when the dawn was bright, Erec prepares to start, commanding his horses to be saddled. His fair sweetheart, too, awakes, dresses, and makes ready. The vavasor and his wife rise too, and every knight and lady there prepares to escort the damsel and the knight. Now they are all on horseback, and the Count as well. Erec rides beside the Count, having beside him his sweetheart ever mindful of her hawk. Having no other riches, she plays with her hawk. Very merry were they as they rode along; but when the time came to part, the Count wished to send along with Erec a party of his knights to do him honour by escorting him. But he announced that none should bide with him, and that he wanted no company but that of the damsel. Then, when they had accompanied them some distance, he said: "In God's name, farewell!" Then the Count kisses Erec and his niece, and commends them both to merciful God. Her father and mother, too, kiss them again and again, and could not keep back their tears: at parting, the mother weeps, the father and the daughter too. For such is love and human nature, and such is affection between parents and children. They wept from sorrow, tenderness, and love which they had for their child; yet they knew full well that their daughter was to fill a place from which great honour would accrue to them. They shed tears of love and pity when they separated from their daughter, but they had no other cause to weep. They knew well enough that eventually they would receive great honour from her marriage. So at parting many a tear was shed, as weeping they commend one another to God, and thus separate without more delay.

Erec quit his host; for he was very anxious to reach the royal court. In his adventure he took great satisfaction; for now he had a lady passing fair, discreet, courteous, and debonair. He could not look at her enough: for the more he looks at her, the more she pleases him. He cannot help giving her a kiss. He is happy to ride by her side, and it does him good to look at her. Long he gazes at her fair hair, her laughing eyes, and her radiant forehead, her nose, her face, and mouth, for all of which gladness fills his heart. He gazes upon her down to the waist, at her chin and her snowy neck, her bosom and sides, her arms and hands. But no less the damsel looks at the vassal with a clear eye and loyal heart, as if they were in competition. They would not have ceased to survey each other even for promise of a reward! A perfect match they were in courtesy, beauty, and gentleness. And they were so alike in quality, manner, and customs, that no one wishing to tell the truth could choose the better of them, nor the fairer, nor the more discreet. Their sentiments, too,

were much alike; so that they were well suited to each other. Thus each steals
the other's heart away. Law or marriage never brought together two such
sweet creatures. And so they rode along until just on the stroke of noon they
approached the castle of Cardigan, where they were both expected. Some of
the first nobles of the court had gone up to look from the upper windows and
see if they could see them. Queen Guinevere ran up, and even the King came
with Kay and Perceval of Wales, and with them my lord Gawain and Tor, the
son of King Ares; Lucan the cupbearer was there, too, and many another
doughty knight. Finally, they espied Erec coming along in company with his
lady. They all knew him well enough from as far as they could see him. The
Queen is greatly pleased, and indeed the whole court is glad of his coming,
because they all love him so. As soon as he was come before the entrance hall,
the King and Queen go down to meet him, all greeting him in God's name.
They welcome Erec and his maiden, commending and praising her great
beauty. And the King himself caught her and lifted her down from her
palfrey. The King was decked in fine array and was then in cheery mood. He
did signal honour to the damsel by taking her hand and leading her up into
the great stone hall. After them Erec and the Queen also went up hand in
hand, and he said to her: "I bring you, lady, my damsel and my sweetheart
dressed in poor garb. As she was given to me, so have I brought her to you.
She is the daughter of a poor vavasor. Through poverty many an honourable
man is brought low: her father, for instance, is gentle and courteous, but he
has little means. And her mother is a very gentle lady, the sister of a rich
Count. She has no lack of beauty or of lineage, that I should not marry her.
It is poverty that has compelled her to wear this white linen garment until
both sleeves are torn at the side. And yet, had it been my desire, she might
have had dresses rich enough. For another damsel, a cousin of hers, wished
to give her a robe of ermine and of spotted or grey silk. But I would not have
her dressed in any other robe until you should have seen her. Gentle lady,
consider the matter now and see what need she has of a fine becoming gown."
And the Queen at once replies: "You have done quite right; it is fitting that
she should have one of my gowns, and I will give her straightway a rich, fair
gown, both fresh and new." The Queen then hastily took her off to her own
private room, and gave orders to bring quickly the fresh tunic and the
greenish-purple mantle, embroidered with little crosses, which had been made
for herself. The one who went at her behest came bringing to her the mantle
and the tunic, which was lined with white ermine even to the sleeves. At the
wrists and on the neck-band there was in truth more than half a mark's
weight of beaten gold, and everywhere set in the gold there were precious

stones of divers colours, indigo and green, blue and dark brown. This tunic
was very rich, but not a writ less precious, I trow, was the mantle. As yet,
there were no ribbons on it; for the mantle like the tunic was brand new. The
mantle was very rich and fine: laid about the neck were two sable skins, and
in the tassels there was more than an ounce of gold; on one a hyacinth, and
on the other a ruby flashed more bright than burning candle. The fur lining
was of white ermine; never was finer seen or found. The cloth was skilfully
embroidered with little crosses, all different, indigo, vermilion, dark blue,
white, green, blue, and yellow. The Queen called for some ribbons four ells
long, made of silken thread and gold. The ribbons are given to her, handsome
and well matched. Quickly she had them fastened to the mantle by some one
who knew how to do it, and who was master of the art. When the mantle
needed no more touches, the gay and gentle lady clasped the maid with the
white gown and said to her cheerily: "Mademoiselle, you must change this
frock for this tunic which is worth more than a hundred marks of silver. So
much I wish to bestow upon you. And put on this mantle, too. Another time
I will give you more." Not able to refuse the gift, she takes the robe and
thanks her for it. Then two maids took her aside into a room, where she took
off her frock as being of no further value; but she asked and requested that it
be given away (to some poor woman) for the love of God. Then she dons the
tunic, and girds herself, binding on tightly a golden belt, and afterwards puts
on the mantle. Now she looked by no means ill; for the dress became her so
well that it made her look more beautiful than ever. The two maids wove a
gold thread in amongst her golden hair: but her tresses were more radiant
than the thread of gold, fine though it was. The maids, moreover, wove a fillet
of flowers of many various colours and placed it upon her head. They strove
as best they might to adorn her in such wise that no fault should be found
with her attire. Strung upon a ribbon around her neck, a damsel hung two
brooches of enamelled gold. Now she looked so charming and fair that I do
not believe that you could find her equal in any land, search as you might, so
skilfully had Nature wrought in her. Then she stepped out of the dress-
ing-room into the Queen's presence. The Queen made much of her, because
she liked her and was glad that she was beautiful and had such gentle
manners. They took each other by the hand and passed into the King's
presence. And when the King saw them, he got up to meet them. When they
came into the great hall, there were so many knights there who rose before
them that I cannot call by name the tenth part of them, or the thirteenth, or
the fifteenth. But I can tell you the names of some of the best of the knights
who belonged to the Round Table and who were the best in the world.

Before all the excellent knights, Gawain ought to be named the first, and second Erec the son of Lac, and third Lancelot of the Lake. Gornemant of Gohort was fourth, and the fifth was the Handsome Coward. The sixth was the Ugly Brave, the seventh Meliant of Liz, the eighth Mauduit the Wise, and the ninth Dodinel the Wild. Let Gandelu be named the tenth, for he was a goodly man. The others I shall mention without order, because the numbers bother me. Eslit was there with Briien, and Yvain the son of Uriien. And Yvain of Loenel was there, as well as Yvain the Adulterer. Beside Yvain of Cavaliot was Garravain of Estrangot. After the Knight with the Horn was the Youth with the Golden Ring. And Tristan who never laughed sat beside Bliobleheris, and beside Brun of Piciez was his brother Gru the Sullen. The Armourer sat next, who preferred war to peace. Next sat Karadues the Shortarmed, a knight of good cheer; and Caveron of Robendic, and the son of King Quenedic and the Youth of Quintareus and Yder of the Dolorous Mount. Gaheriet and Kay of Estraus, Amauguin and Gales the Bald, Grain, Gornevain, and Carabes, and Tor the son of King Aras, Girflet the son of Do, and Taulas, who never wearied of arms: and a young man of great merit, Loholt the son of King Arthur, and Sagremor the Impetuous, who should not be forgotten, nor Bedoiier the Master of the Horse, who was skilled at chess and trictrac, nor Bravain, nor King Lot, nor Galegantin of Wales, nor Gronosis, versed in evil, who was son of Kay the Seneschal, nor Labigodes the Courteous, nor Count Cadorcaniois, nor Letron of Prepelesant, whose manners were so excellent, nor Breon the son of Canodan, nor the Count of Honolan who had such a head of fine fair hair; he it was who received the King's horn in an evil day; he never had any care for truth.

When the stranger maiden saw all the knights arrayed looking steadfastly at her, she bowed her head in embarrassment; nor was it strange that her face blushed all crimson. But her confusion was so becoming to her that she looked all the more lovely. When the King saw that she was embarrassed, he did not wish to leave her side. Taking her gently by the hand, he made her sit down on his right hand; and on his left sat the Queen, speaking thus to the King the while. "Sire, in my opinion he who can win such a fair lady by his arms in another land ought by right to come to a royal court. It was well we waited for Erec; for now you can bestow the kiss upon the fairest of the court. I should think none would find fault with you! for none can say, unless he lie, that this maiden is not the most charming of all the damsels here, or indeed in all the world." The King makes answer: "That is no lie; and upon her, if there is no remonstrance, I shall bestow the honour of the White Stag." Then he added to the knights: "My lords, what say you? What is your opinion? In body, in face, and in whatever a maid should have, this one is the most charming and beautiful to be found, as I may say, before you come to where Heaven and earth meet. I say it is meet that she should receive the honour of the Stag. And you, my lords, what do you think about it? Can you make any objection? If any one wishes to protest, let him straightway speak his mind. I am King, and must keep my word and must not permit any baseness, falsity, or arrogance. I must maintain truth and righteousness. It is the business of a loyal king to support the law, truth, faith, and justice. I would not in any wise commit a disloyal deed or wrong to either weak or strong. It is not meet that any one should complain of me; nor do I wish the custom and the practice to lapse, which my family has been wont to foster. You, too, would doubtless regret to see me strive to introduce other customs and other laws than those my royal sire observed. Regardless of consequences, I am bound to keep and maintain the institution of my father Pendragon, who was a just king and emperor. Now tell me fully what you think! Let none be slow to speak his mind, if this damsel is not the fairest of my household and ought not by right to receive the kiss of the White Stag: I wish to know what you truly think." Then they all cry with one accord: "Sire, by the Lord and his Cross! you may well kiss her with good reason, for she is the fairest one there is. In this damsel there is more beauty than there is of radiance in the sun. You may kiss her freely, for we all agree in sanctioning it." When the King hears that this is well pleasing to them all, he will no longer delay in bestowing the kiss, but turns toward her and embraces her. The maid was sensible, and perfectly willing that the King should kiss her; she would have been discourteous, indeed, to resent it. In courteous fashion and in the presence of all his knights the King kissed her, and said: "My dear. I give you my love in all honesty. I will love you with true heart, without malice and without guile." By this adventure the King carried out the practice and the usage to which the White Stag was entitled at his court.

Here ends the first part of my story.

When the kiss of the Stag was taken according to the custom of the country, Erec, like a polite and kind man, was solicitous for his poor host. It was not his intention to fail to execute what he had promised. Hear how he kept his covenant: for he sent him now five sumpter mules, strong and sleek, loaded with dresses and clothes, buckrams and scarlets, marks of gold and silver plate, furs both vair and grey, skins of sable, purple stuffs, and silks. When the mules were loaded with all that a gentleman can need, he sent with them an escort of ten knights and sergeants chosen from his own men, and straightly charged them to salute his host and show great honour both to him and to his lady, as if it were to himself in person; and when they should have presented to them the sumpters which they brought them, the gold, the silver, and money, and all the other furnishings which were in the boxes, they should escort the lady and the vavasor with great honour into his kingdom of Farther Wales. Two towns there he had promised them, the most choice and the best situated that there were in all his land, with nothing to fear from attack. Montrevel was the name of one, and the other's name was Roadan. When they should arrive in his kingdom, they should make over to them these two towns, together with their rents and their jurisdiction, in accordance with what he had promised them. All was carried out as Erec had ordered. The messengers made no delay, and in good time they presented to his host the gold and the silver and the sumpters and the robes and the money, of which there was great plenty. They escorted them into Erec's kingdom, and strove to serve them well. They came into the country on the third day, and transferred to them the towers of the towns; for King Lac made no objection. He gave them a warm welcome and showed them honour, loving them for the sake of his son Erec. He made over to them the title to the towns, and established their suzerainty by making knights and bourgeois swear that they would reverence them as their true liege lords. When this was done and accomplished, the messengers returned to their lord Erec, who received them gladly. When he asked for news of the vavasor and his lady, of his own father and of his kingdom, the report they gave him was good and fair.

Not long after this, the time drew near when Erec was to celebrate his marriage. The delay was irksome to him, and he resolved no longer to suffer and wait. So he went and asked of the King that it might please him to allow him to be married at the court. The King vouchsafed him the boon, and sent through all his kingdom to search for the kings and counts who were his liege-men, bidding them that none be so bold as not to be present at Pentecost. None dares to hold back and not go to court at the King's summons. Now I will tell you, and listen well, who were these counts and kings. With a rich escort and one hundred extra mounts Count Brandes of Gloucester came. After him came Menagormon, who was Count of Clivelon. And he of the Haute Montagne came with a very rich following. The Count of Treverain came, too, with a hundred of his knights, and Count Godegrain with as many more. Along with those whom I have just mentioned came Maheloas, a great baron, lord of the Isle of Voirre. In this island no thunder is heard, no lightning strikes, nor tempests rage, nor do toads or serpents exist there, nor is it ever too hot or too cold. Graislemier of Fine Posterne brought twenty companions, and had with him his brother Guigomar, lord of the Isle of Avalon. Of the latter we have heard it said that he was a friend of Morgan the Fay, and such he was in very truth. Davit of Tintagel came, who never suffered woe or grief. Guergesin, the Duke of Haut Bois, came with a very rich equipment. There was no lack of counts and dukes, but of kings there were still more. Garras of Cork, a doughty king, was there with five hundred knights clad in mantles, hose, and tunics of brocade and silk. Upon a Cappadocian steed came Aguisel, the Scottish king, and brought with him his two sons, Cadret and Coi—two much respected knights. Along with those whom I have named came King Ban of Gomeret, and he had in his company only young men, beardless as yet on chin and lip. A numerous and gay band he brought two hundred of them in his suite; and there was none, whoever he be, but had a falcon or tercel, a merlin or a sparrow-hawk, or some precious pigeon-hawk, golden or mewed. Kerrin, the old King of Riel, brought no youth, but rather three hundred companions of whom the youngest was seven score years old. Because of their great age, their heads were all as white as snow, and their beards reached down to their girdles. Arthur held them in great respect. The lord of the dwarfs came next, Bilis, the king of Antipodes. This king of whom I speak was a dwarf himself and own brother of Brien. Bilis, on the one hand, was the smallest of all the dwarfs, while his brother Brien was a half-foot or full palm taller than any other knight in the kingdom. To display his wealth and power, Bilis brought with him two kings who were also dwarfs and who were vassals of his, Grigoras and Glecidalan. Every one looked at them as marvels. When they had arrived at court, they were treated with great esteem. All three were honoured and served at the court like kings, for they were very perfect gentlemen. In brief, when King Arthur saw all his lords assembled, his heart was glad. Then, to heighten the joy, he ordered a hundred squires to be bathed whom he wished to dub knights. There was none of them but had a parti-coloured robe of rich brocade of Alexandria, each one choosing such as pleased his fancy. All had arms of a uniform pattern, and horses swift and full of mettle, of which the worst was worth a hundred livres.

When Erec received his wife, he must needs call her by her right name. For a wife is not espoused unless she is called by her proper name. As yet no one knew her name, but now for the first time it was made known: Enide was her baptismal name. The Archbishop of Canterbury, who had come to the court, blessed them, as is his right. When the court was all assembled, there was not a minstrel in the countryside who possessed any pleasing accomplishment that did not come to the court. In the great hall there was much merry-making, each one contributing what he could to the entertainment: one jumps, another tumbles, another does magic; there is story-telling, singing, whistling, playing from notes; they play on the harp, the rote, the fiddle, the violin, the flute, and pipe. The maidens sing and dance, and outdo each other in the merry-making. At the wedding that day everything was done which can give joy and incline man's heart to gladness. Drums are beaten, large and small, and there is playing of pipes, fifes, horns, trumpets, and bagpipes. What more shall I say? There was not a wicket or a gate kept closed; but the exits and entrances all stood ajar, so that no one, poor or rich, was turned away. King Arthur was not miserly, but gave orders to the bakers, the cooks, and the butlers that they should serve every one generously with bread, wine, and venison. No one asked anything whatever to be passed to him without getting all he desired.

There was great merriment in the palace. But I will pass over the rest, and you shall hear of the joy and pleasure in the bridal chamber. Bishops and archbishops were there on the night when the bride and groom retired. At this their first meeting, Iseut was not filched away, nor was Brangien put in her place. The Queen herself took charge of their preparations for the night; for both of them were dear to her. The hunted stag which pants for thirst does not so long for the spring, nor does the hungry sparrow-hawk return so quickly when he is called, as did these two come to hold each other in close embrace. That night they had full compensation for their long delay. After the chamber had been cleared, they allow each sense to be gratified: the eyes, which are the entrance-way of love, and which carry messages to the heart, take satisfaction in the glance, for they rejoice in all they see; after the message of the eyes comes the far surpassing sweetness of the kisses inviting love; both of them make trial of this sweetness, and let their hearts quaff so freely that hardly can they leave off. Thus, kissing was their first sport. And the love which is between them emboldened the maid and left her quite without her fears; regardless of pain, she suffered all. Before she rose, she no longer bore the name of maid; in the morning she was a new-made dame. That day the minstrels were in happy mood, for they were all well paid. They were fully compensated for the entertainment they had given, and many a handsome gift was bestowed upon them: robes of grey squirrel skin and ermine, of rabbit skins and violet stuffs, scarlets and silken stuffs. Whether it be a horse or money, each one got what he deserved according to his skill. And thus the wedding festivities and the court lasted almost a fortnight with great joy and magnificence. For his own glory and satisfaction, as well as to honour Erec the more, King Arthur made all the knights remain a full fortnight. When the third week began, all together by common consent agreed to hold a tournament. On the one side, my lord Gawain offered himself as surety that it would take place between Evroic and Tenebroc: and Meliz and Meliadoc were guarantors on the other side. Then the court separated.

A month after Pentecost the tournament assembled, and the jousting began in the plain below Tenebroc. Many an ensign of red, blue, and white, many a veil and many a sleeve were bestowed as tokens of love. Many a lance was carried there, flying the colours argent and green, or gold and azure blue. There were many, too, with different devices, some with stripes and some with dots. That day one saw laced on many a helmet of gold or steel, some green, some yellow, and others red, all aglowing in the sun; so many scutcheons and white hauberks; so many swords girt on the left side; so many good shields, fresh and new, some resplendent in silver and green, others of azure with buckles of gold; so many good steeds marked with white, or sorrel, tawny, white, black, and bay: all gather hastily. And now the field is quite covered with arms. On either side the ranks tremble, and a roar rises from the fight. The shock of the lances is very great. Lances break and shields are riddled, the hauberks receive bumps and are torn asunder, saddles go empty and horsemen ramble, while the horses sweat and foam. Swords are quickly drawn on those who tumble noisily, and some run to receive the promise of a ransom, others to stave off this disgrace. Erec rode a white horse, and came forth alone at the head of the line to joust, if he may find an opponent. From the opposite side there rides out to meet him Orguelleus de la Lande, mounted on an Irish steed which bears him along with marvellous speed. On the shield before his breast Erec strikes him with such force that he knocks him from his horse: he leaves him prone and passes on. Then Raindurant opposed him, son of the old dame of Tergalo, covered with blue cloth of silk; he was a knight of great prowess. Against one another now they charge and deal fierce blows on the shields about their neck. Erec from lance's length lays him over on the hard ground. While riding back he met the King of the Red City, who was very valiant and bold. They grasp their reins by the knots and their shields by the inner straps. They both had fine arms, and strong swift horses, and good shields, fresh and new. With such fury they strike each other that both their lances fly in splinters. Never was there seen such a blow. They rush together with shields, arms, and horses. But neither girth nor rein nor breast-strap could prevent the king from coming to earth. So he flew from his steed, carrying with him saddle and stirrup, and even the reins of his bridle in his hand. All those who witnessed the jousting were filled with amazement, and said it cost him dear to joust with such a goodly knight. Erec did not wish to stop to capture either horse or rider, but rather to joust and distinguish himself in order that his prowess might appear. He thrills the ranks in front of him. Gawain animates those who were on his side by his prowess, and by winning horses and knights to the discomfiture of his opponents. I speak of my lord Gawain, who did right well and valiantly. In the fight he unhorsed Guincel, and took Gaudin of the Mountain; he captured knights and horses alike: my lord Gawain did well. Girtlet the son of Do, and Yvain, and Sagremor the Impetuous, so evilly entreated their adversaries that they drove them back to the gates, capturing and unhorsing many of them. In front of the gate of the town the strife began again between those within and those without. There Sagremor was thrown down, who was a very gallant knight. He was on the point of being detained and captured, when Erec spurs to rescue him, breaking his lance into splinters upon one of the opponents. So hard he strikes him on the breast that he made him quit the saddle. Then he made of his sword and advances upon them, crushing and splitting their helmets. Some flee, and others make way before him, for even the boldest fears him. Finally, he distributed so many blows and thrusts that he rescued Sagremor from them, and drove them all in confusion into the town. Meanwhile, the vesper hour drew to a close. Erec bore himself so well that day that he was the best of the combatants. But on the morrow he did much better yet: for he took so many knights and left so many saddles empty that none could believe it except those who had seen it. Every one on both sides said that with his lance and shield he had won the honours of the tournament. Now was Erec's renown so high that no one spoke save of him, nor was any one of such goodly favour. In countenance he resembled Absalom, in language he seemed a Solomon, in boldness he equalled Samson, and in generous giving and spending he was the equal of Alexander. On his return from the tourney Erec went to speak with the King. He went to ask him for leave to go and visit his own land; but first he thanked him like a frank, wise, and courteous man for the honour which he had done him; for very deep was his gratitude. Then he asked his permission to leave, for he wished to visit his own country, and he wished to take his wife with him. This request the King could not deny, and yet he would have had him stay. He gives him leave and begs him to return as soon as possible: for in the whole court there was no better or more gallant knight, save only his dear nephew Gawain; with him no one could be compared. But next after him, he prized Erec most, and held him more dear than any other knight.

Erec wished to delay no longer. As soon as he had the King's leave, he bid his wife make her preparations, and he retained as his escort sixty knights of merit with horses and with dappled and grey furs. As soon as he was ready for his journey, he tarried little further at court, but took leave of the Queen and commended the knights to God. The Queen grants him leave to depart. At the hour of prime he set out from the royal palace. In the presence of them all he mounted his steed, and his wife mounted the dappled horse which she had brought from her own country; then all his escort mounted. Counting knights and squires, there were full seven score in the train. After four long days' journey over hills and slopes, through forests, plains, and streams, they came on the fifth day to Camant, where King Lac was residing in a very charming town. No one ever saw one better situated; for the town was provided with forests and meadow-land, with vineyards and farms, with streams and orchards, with ladies and knights, and fine, lively youths, and polite, well-mannered clerks who spent their incomes freely, with fair and charming maidens, and with prosperous burghers. Before Erec reached the town, he sent two knights ahead to announce his arrival to the King. When he heard the news, the King had clerks, knights, and damsels quickly mount, and ordered the bells to be rung, and the streets to be hung with tapestries and silken stuffs, that his son might be received with joy; then he himself got on his horse. Of clerks there were present fourscore, gentle and honourable men, clad in grey cloaks bordered with sable. Of knights there were full five hundred, mounted on bay, sorrel, or white-spotted steeds. There were so many burghers and dames that no one could tell the number of them. The King and his son galloped and rode on till they saw and recognised each other. They both jump down from their horses and embrace and greet each other for a long time, without stirring from the place where they first met. Each party wished the other joy: the King makes much of Erec, but all at once breaks off to turn to Enide. On all sides he is in clover: he embraces and kisses them both, and knows not which of the two pleases him the more. As they gaily enter the castle, the bells all ring their peals to honour Erec's arrival. The streets are all strewn with reeds, mint, and iris, and are hung overhead with curtains and tapestries of fancy silk and satin stuffs. There was great rejoicing; for all the people came together to see their new lord, and no one ever saw greater happiness than was shown alike by young and old. First they came to the church, where very devoutly they were received in a procession. Erec kneeled before the altar of the Crucifix, and two knights led his wife to the image of Our Lady. When she had finished her prayer, she stepped back a little and crossed herself with her right hand, as a well-bred dame should do.

Then they came out from the church and entered the royal palace, when the festivity began. That day Erec received many presents from the knights and burghers: from one a palfrey of northern stock, and from another a golden cup. One presents him with a golden pigeon-hawk, another with a setter-dog, this one a greyhound, this other a sparrowhawk, and another a swift Arab steed, this one a shield, this one an ensign, this one a sword, and this a helmet. Never was a king more gladly seen in his kingdom, nor received with greater joy, as all strove to serve him well. Yet greater joy they made of Enide than of him, for the great beauty which they saw in her, and still more for her open charm. She was seated in a chamber upon a cushion of brocade which had been brought from Thessaly. Round about her was many a fair lady; yet as the lustrous gem outshines the brown flint, and as the rose excels the poppy, so was Enide fairer than any other lady or damsel to be found in the world, wherever one might search. She was so gentle and honourable, of wise speech and affable, of pleasing character and kindly mien. No one could ever be so watchful as to detect in her any folly, or sign of evil or villainy. She had been so schooled in good manners that she had learned all virtues which any lady can possess, as well as generosity and knowledge. All loved her for her open heart, and whoever could do her any service was glad and esteemed himself the more. No one spoke any ill of her, for no one could do so. In the realm or empire there was no lady of such good manners. But Erec loved her with such a tender love that he cared no more for arms, nor did he go to tournaments, nor have any desire to joust; but he spent his time in cherishing his wife. He made of her his mistress and his sweetheart. He devoted all his heart and mind to fondling and kissing her, and sought no delight in other pastime. His friends grieved over this, and often regretted among themselves that he was so deep in love. Often it was past noon before he left her side; for there he was happy, say what they might. He rarely left her society, and yet he was as open-handed as ever to his knights with arms, dress, and money. There was not a tournament anywhere to which he did not send them well apparelled and equipped. Whatever the cost might be, he gave them fresh steeds for the tourney and joust. All the knights said it was a great pity and misfortune that such a valiant man as he was wont to be should no longer wish to bear arms. He was blamed so much on all sides by the knights and squires that murmurs reached Enide's ears how that her lord had turned craven about arms and deeds of chivalry, and that his manner of life was greatly changed. She grieved sorely over this, but she did not dare to show her grief; for her lord at once would take affront, if she should speak to him. So the matter remained a secret, until one morning they lay in bed where they had had sport together. There they lay in close embrace, like the true lovers they were. He was asleep, but she was awake, thinking of what many a man in the country was saying of her lord. And when she began to think it all over, she could not keep back the tears. Such was her grief and her chagrin that by mischance she let fall a word for which she later felt remorse, though in her heart there was no guile. She began to survey her lord from head to foot, his well-shaped body and his clear countenance, until her tears fell fast upon the bosom of her lord, and she said: "Alas, woe is me that I ever left my country! What did I come here to seek? The earth ought by right to swallow me up when the best knight, the most hardy, brave, fair, and courteous that ever was a count or king, has completely abjured all his deeds of chivalry because of me. And thus, in truth, it is I who have brought shame upon his head, though I would fain not have done so at any price." Then she said to him: "Unhappy thou!" And then kept silence and spoke no more. Erec was not sound asleep and, though dozing, heard plainly what she said. He aroused at her words, and much surprised to see her weeping, he asked her: "Tell me, my precious beauty, why do you weep thus? What has caused you woe or sorrow? Surely it is my wish to know. Tell me now, my gentle sweetheart; and raise care to keep nothing back, why you said that woe was me? For you said it of me and of no one else. I heard your words plainly enough." Then was Enide in a great plight, afraid and dismayed. "Sire," says she, "I know nothing of what you say." "Lady, why do you conceal it? Concealment is of no avail. You hare been crying; I can see that, and you do not cry for nothing. And in my sleep I heard what you said." "Ah! fair sire, you never heard it, and I dare say it was a dream." "Now you are coming to me with lies. I hear you calmly lying to me. But if you do not tell me the truth now, you will come to repent of it later." "Sire, since you torment me thus, I will tell you the whole truth, and keep nothing back. But I am afraid that you will not like it. In this land they all say—the dark, the fair, and the ruddy—that it is a great pity that you should renounce your arms; your reputation has suffered from it. Every one used to say not long ago that in all the world there was known no better or more gallant knight. Now they all go about making game of you—old and young, little and great—calling you a recreant. Do you suppose it does not give me pain to hear you thus spoken of with scorn? It grieves me when I hear it said, and yet it grieves me more that they put the blame for it on me. Yes, I am blamed for it, I regret to say, and they all assert it is because I have so ensnared and caught you that you are losing all your merit, and do not care for aught but me. You must choose another course, so that you may silence this reproach and regain your former fame; for I have heard too much of this reproach, and yet I did not dare to disclose it to you. Many a time, when I think of it, I have to weep for very grief. Such chagrin I felt just now that I could not keep myself from saying that you were ill-starred." "Lady," said he, "you were in the right, and those who blame me do so with reason. And now at once prepare yourself to take the road. Rise up from here, and dress yourself in your richest robe, and order your saddle to be put on your best palfrey." Now Enide is in great distress: very sad and pensive, she gets up, blaming and upbraiding herself for the foolish words she spoke: she had now made her bed, and must lie in it. "Ah!" said she, "poor fool! I was too happy, for there lacked me nothing. God! why was I so forward as to dare to utter such folly? God! did not my lord love me to excess? In faith, alas, he was too fond of me. And now I must go away into exile. But I have yet a greater grief, that I shall no longer see my lord, who loved me with such tenderness that there was nothing he held so dear. The best man that was ever born had become so wrapped up in me that he cared for nothing else. I lacked for nothing then. I was very happy. But pride it is that stirred me up: because of my pride, I must suffer woe for telling him such insulting words, and it is right that I should suffer woe. One does not know what good fortune is until he has made trial of evil." Thus the lady bemoaned her fate, while she dressed herself fitly in her richest robe. Yet nothing gave her any pleasure, but rather cause for deep chagrin. Then she had a maid call one of her squires, and bids him saddle her precious palfrey of northern stock, than which no count or king ever had a better. As soon as she had given him the command, the fellow asked for no delay, but straightway went and saddled the dappled palfrey. And Erec summoned another squire and bade him bring his arms to arm his body withal. Then he went up into a bower, and had a Limoges rug laid out before him on the floor. Meanwhile, the squire ran to fetch the arms and came back and laid them on the rug. Erec took a seat opposite, on the figure of a leopard which was portrayed on the rug. He prepares and gets ready to put on his arms: first, he had laced on a pair of greaves of polished steel; next, he dons a hauberk, which was so fine that not a mesh could be cut away from it. This hauberk of his was rich, indeed, for neither inside nor outside of it was there enough iron to make a needle, nor could it gather any rust; for it was all made of worked silver in tiny meshes triple-wove; and it was made with such skill that I can assure you that no one who had put it on would have been more uncomfortable or sore because of it, than if he had put on a silk jacket over his undershirt. The knights and squires all began to wonder why he was being armed; but no one dared to ask him why. When they had put on his hauberk, a valet laces about his head a helmet fluted with a band of gold, shining brighter than a mirror. Then he takes the sword and girds it on, and orders them to bring him saddled his bay steed of Gascony. Then he calls a valet to him, and says: "Valet, go quickly, run to the chamber beside the tower where my wife is, and tell her that she is keeping me waiting here too long. She has spent too much time on her attire. Tell her to come and mount at once, for I am awaiting her." And the fellow goes and finds her all ready, weeping and making moan: and he straightway addressed her thus: "Lady, why do you so delay? My lord is awaiting you outside yonder, already fully armed. He would have mounted some time ago, had you been ready." Enide wondered greatly what her lord's intention was; but she very wisely showed herself with as cheerful a countenance as possible, when she appeared before him. In the middle of the courtyard she found him, and King Lac comes running out. Knights come running, too, striving with each other to reach there first. There is neither young nor old but goes to learn and ask if he will take any of them with him. So each offers and presents himself. But he states definitely and affirms that he will take no companion except his wife, asserting that he will go alone. Then the King is in great distress. "Fair son," says he, "what dost thou intend to do? Thou shouldst tell me thy business and keep nothing back. Tell me whither thou will go; for thou art unwilling on any account to be accompanied by an escort of squires or knights. If thou hast undertaken to fight some knight in single combat, yet shouldst thou not for that reason fail to take a part of thy knights with thee to betoken thy wealth and lordship. A king's son ought not to fare alone. Fair son, have thy sumpters loaded now, and take thirty or forty or more of thy knights, and see that silver and gold is taken, and whatever a gentleman needs." Finally Erec makes reply and tells him all in detail how he has planned his journey. "Sire," says he, "it must be so. I shall take no extra horse, nor have I any use for gold or silver, squire or sergeant; nor do I ask for any company save that of my wife alone. But I pray you, whatever may happen, should I die and she come back, to love her and hold her dear for love of me and for my prayer, and give her so long as she live, without contention or any strife, the half of your land to be her own." Upon hearing his son's request, the King said: "Fair son, I promise it. But I grieve much to see thee thus go off without escort, and if I had my way, thou shouldst not thus depart." "Sire, it cannot be otherwise. I go now, and to God commend you. But keep in mind my companions, and give them horses and arms and all that knight may need." The King cannot keep back the tears when he is parted from his son. The people round about weep too; the ladies and knights shed tears and make great moan for him. There is not one who does not mourn, and many a one in the courtyard swoons. Weeping, they kiss and embrace him, and are almost beside themselves with grief. I think they would not have been more sad if they had seen him dead or wounded. Then Erec said to comfort them: "My lords, why do you weep so sore? I am neither in prison nor wounded. You gain nothing by this display of grief. If I go away, I shall come again when it please God and when I can. To God I commend you one and all; so now let me go; too long you keep me here. I am sorry and grieved to see you weep." To God he commends them and they him.

So they departed, leaving sorrow behind them. Erec starts, and leads his wife he knows not whither, as chance dictates. "Ride fast," he says, "and take good care not to be so rash as to speak to me of anything you may see. Take care never to speak to me, unless I address you first. Ride on now fast and with confidence." "Sire," says she, "it shall be done." She rode ahead and held her peace. Neither one nor the other spoke a word. But Enide's heart is very sad, and within herself she thus laments, soft and low that he may not hear: "Alas," she says, "God had raised and exalted me to such great joy; but now He has suddenly cast me down. Fortune who had beckoned me has quickly now withdrawn her hand. I should not mind that so much, alas, if only I dared to address my lord. But I am mortified and distressed because my lord has turned against me, I see it clearly, since he will not speak to me. And I am not so bold as to dare to look at him." While she thus laments, a knight who lived by robbery issued forth from the woods. He had two companions with him, and all three were armed. They covet the palfrey which Enide rides. "My lords, do you know the news I bring?" says he to his two companions. "If we do not now make a haul, we are good-for-nothing cowards and are playing in bad luck. Here comes a lady wondrous fair, whether married or not I do not know, but she is very richly dressed. The palfrey and saddle, with the breast-strap and reins, are worth a thousand livres of Chartres. I will take the palfrey for mine, and the rest of the booty you may have. I don't want any more for my share. The knight shall not lead away the lady, so help me God. For I intend to give him such a thrust as he will dearly pay. I it was who saw him first, and so it is my right to go the first and offer battle." They give him leave and he rides off, crouching well beneath his shield, while the other two remain aloof. In those days it was the custom and practice that in an attack two knights should not join against one; thus if they too had assailed him, it would seem that they had acted treacherously. Enide saw the robbers, and was seized with great fear. "God," says she, "what can I say? Now my lord will be either killed or made a prisoner; for there are three of them and he is alone. The contest is not fair between one knight and three. That fellow will strike him now at a disadvantage; for my lord is off his guard. God, shall I be then such a craven as not to dare to raise my voice? Such a coward I will not be: I will not fail to speak to him." On the spot she turns about and calls to him: "Fair sire, of what are you thinking? There come riding after you three knights who press you hard. I greatly fear they will do you harm." "What?" says Erec, "what's that you say? You have surely been very bold to disdain my command and prohibition. This time you shall be pardoned; but if it should happen another time, you would not be forgiven." Then turning his shield and lance, he rushes at the knight. The latter sees him coming and challenges him. When Erec hears him, he defies him. Both give spur and clash together, holding their lances at full extent. But he missed Erec, while Erec used him hard; for he knew well the right attack. He strikes him on the shield so fiercely that he cracks it from top to bottom. Nor is his hauberk any protection: Erec pierces and crushes it in the middle of his breast, and thrusts a foot and a half of his lance into his body. When he drew back, he pulled out the shaft. And the other fell to earth. He must needs die, for the blade had drunk of his life's blood. Then one of the other two rushes forward, leaving his companion behind, and spurs toward Erec, threatening him. Erec firmly grasps his shield, and attacks him with a stout heart. The other holds his shield before his breast. Then they strike upon the emblazoned shields. The knight's lance flies into two bits, while Erec drives a quarter of lance's length through the other's breast. He will give him no more trouble. Erec unhorses him and leaves him in a faint, while he spurs at an angle toward the third robber. When the latter saw him coming on he began to make his escape. He was afraid, and did not dare to face him; so he hastened to take refuge in the woods. But his flight is of small avail, for Erec follows him close and cries aloud: "Vassal, vassal, turn about now, and prepare to defend yourself, so that I may not slay you in act of flight. It is useless to try to escape." But the fellow has no desire to turn about, and continues to flee with might and main. Following and overtaking him, Erec hits him squarely on his painted shield, and throws him over on the other side. To these three robbers he gives no further heed: one he has killed, another wounded, and of the third he got rid by throwing him to earth from his steed. He took the horses of all three and tied them together by the bridles. In colour they were not alike: the first was white as milk, the second black and not at all bad looking, while the third was dappled all over. He came back to the road where Enide was awaiting him. He bade her lead and drive the three horses in front of her, warning her harshly never again to be so bold as to speak a single word unless he give her leave. She makes answer: "I will never do so, fair sire, if it be your will." Then they ride on, and she holds her peace.

They had not yet gone a league when before them in a valley there came five other knights, with lances in rest, shields held close in to the neck, and their shining helmets laced up tight; they, too, were on plunder bent. All at once they saw the lady approach in charge of the three horses, and Erec who followed after. As soon as they saw them, they divided their equipment among themselves, just as if they had already taken possession of it. Covetousness is a bad thing. But it did not turn out as they expected; for vigorous defence was made. Much that a fool plans is not executed, and many a man misses what he thinks to obtain. So it befell them in this attack. One said that he would take the maid or lose his life in the attempt; and another said that the dappled steed shall be his, and that he will be satisfied with that. The third said that he would take the black horse. "And the white one for me," said the fourth. The fifth was not at all backward, and vowed that he would have the horse and arms of the knight himself. He wished to win them by himself, and would fain attack him first, if they would give him leave: and they willingly gave consent. Then he leaves them and rides ahead on a good and nimble steed. Erec saw him, but made pretence that he did not yet notice him. When Enide saw them, her heart jumped with fear and great dismay. "Alas!" said she, "I know not what to say or do; for my lord severely threatens me, and says that he will punish me, if I speak a word to him. But if my lord were dead now, there would be no comfort for me. I should be killed and roughly treated. God! my lord does not see them! Why, then, do I hesitate, crazed as I am? I am indeed too chary of my words, when I have not already spoken to him. I know well enough that those who are coming yonder are intent upon some wicked deed. And God! how shall I speak to him? He will kill me. Well, let him kill me! Yet I will not fail to speak to him." Then she softly calls him: "Sire!" "What?" says he, "what do you want?" "Your pardon, sire. I want to tell you that five knights have emerged from yonder thicket, of whom I am in mortal fear. Having noticed them, I am of the opinion that they intend to fight with you. Four of them have stayed behind, and the other comes toward you as fast as his steed can carry him. I am afraid every moment lest he will strike you. 'Tis true, the four have stayed behind; but still they are not far away, and will quickly aid him, if need arise." Erec replies: "You had an evil thought, when you transgressed my command—a thing which I had forbidden you. And yet I knew all the time that you did not hold me in esteem. Your service has been ill employed; for it has not awakened my gratitude, but rather kindled the more my ire. I have told you that once, and I say it again. This once again I will pardon you; but another time restrain yourself, and do not again turn around to watch me: for in doing so you would be very foolish. I do not relish your words." Then he spurs across the field toward his adversary, and they come together. Each seeks out and assails the other. Erec strikes him with such force that his shield flies from his neck, and thus he breaks his collar-bone. His stirrups break, and he falls without the strength to rise again, for he was badly bruised and wounded. One of the others then appeared, and they attack each other fiercely. Without difficulty Erec thrusts the sharp and well forged steel into his neck beneath the chin, severing thus the bones and nerves. At the back of his neck the blade protrudes, and the hot red blood flows down on both sides from the wound. He yields his spirit, and his heart is still. The third sallies forth from his hiding-place on the other side of a ford. Straight through the water, on he comes. Erec spurs forward and meets him before he came out of the water, striking him so hard that he beats down flat both rider and horse. The steed lay upon the body long enough to drown him in the stream, and then struggled until with difficulty he got upon his feet. Thus he conquered three of them, when the other two thought it wise to quit the conflict and not to strive with him. In flight they follow the stream, and Erec after them in hot pursuit, until he strikes one upon the spine so hard that he throws him forward upon the saddle-bow. He put all his strength into the blow, and breaks his lance upon his body, so that the fellow fell head foremost. Erec makes him pay dearly for the lance which he has broken on him, and drew his sword from the scabbard. The fellow unwisely straightened up; for Erec gave him three such strokes that he slaked his sword's thirst in his blood. He severs the shoulder from his body, so that it fell down on the ground. Then, with sword drawn, he attacked the other, as he sought to escape without company or escort. When he sees Erec pursuing him, he is so afraid that he knows not what to do: he does not dare to face him, and cannot turn aside; he has to leave his horse, for he has no more trust in him. He throws away his shield and lance, and slips from his horse to earth. When he saw him on his feet, Erec no longer cared to pursue him, but he stooped over for the lance, not wishing to leave that, because of his own which had been broken. He carries off his lance and goes away, not leaving the horses behind: he catches all five of them and leads them off. Enide had hard work to lead them all; for he hands over all five of them to her with the other three, and commands her to go along smartly, and to keep from addressing him in order that no evil or harm may come to her. So not a word does she reply, but rather keeps silence; and thus they go, leading with them all the eight horses.

They rode till nightfall without coming to any town or shelter. When night came on, they took refuge beneath a tree in an open field. Erec bids his lady sleep, and he will watch. She replies that she will not, for it is not right, and she does not wish to do so. It is for him to sleep who is more weary. Well pleased at this, Erec accedes. Beneath his head he placed his shield, and the lady took her cloak, and stretched it over him from head to foot. Thus, he slept and she kept watch, never dozing the whole night, but holding tight in her hand by the bridle the horses until the morning broke; and much she blamed and reproached herself for the words which she had uttered, and said that she acted badly, and was not half so ill-treated as she deserved to be. "Alas," said she, "in what an evil hour have I witnessed my pride and presumption! I might have known without doubt that there was no knight better than, or so good as, my lord. I knew it well enough before, but now I know it better. For I have seen with my own eyes how he has not quailed before three or even five armed men. A plague for ever upon my tongue for having uttered such pride and insult as now compel me to suffer shame!" All night long she thus lamented until the morning dawned. Erec rises early, and again they take the road, she in front and he behind. At noon a squire met them in a little valley, accompanied by two fellows who were carrying cakes and wine and some rich autumn cheeses to those who were mowing the hay in the meadows belonging to Count Galoain. The squire was a clever fellow, and when he saw Erec and Enide, who were coming from the direction of the woods, he perceived that they must have spent the night in the forest and had had nothing to eat or drink; for within a radius of a day's journey there was no town, city or tower, no strong place or abbey, hospice or place of refuge. So he formed an honest purpose and turned his steps toward them, saluting them politely and saving: "Sire, I presume that you have had a hard experience last night. I am sure you have had no sleep and have spent the night in these woods. I offer you some of this white cake, if it please you to partake of it. I say it not in hope of reward: for I ask and demand nothing of you. The cakes are made of good wheat; I have good wine and rich cheeses, too, a white cloth and fine jugs. If you feel like taking lunch, you need not seek any farther. Beneath these white beeches, here on the greensward, you might lay off your arms and rest yourself a while. My advice is that you dismount." Erec got down from his horse and said: "Fair gentle friend, I thank you kindly: I will eat something, without going farther." The young man knew well what to do: he helped the lady from her horse, and the boys who had come with the squire held the steeds. Then they go and sit down in the shade. The squire relieves Erec of his helmet, unlaces the mouth-piece from before his face; then he spreads out the cloth before them on the thick tuff. He passes them the cake and wine, and prepares and cuts a cheese. Hungry as they were, they helped themselves, and gladly drank of the wine. The squire serves them and omits no attention. When they had eaten and drunk their fill, Erec was courteous and generous. "Friend," says he, "as a reward, I wish to present you with one of my horses. Take the one you like the best. And I pray it may be no hardship for you to return to the town and make ready there a goodly lodging." And he replies that he will gladly do whatever is his will. Then he goes up to the horses and, untying them, chooses the dapple, and speaks his thanks; for this one seems to be the best. Up he springs by the left stirrup, and leaving them both there, he rode off to the town at top speed, where he engaged suitable quarters. Now behold! he is back again: "Now mount, sire, quickly," says he, "for you have a good fine lodging ready." Erec mounted, and then his lady, and, as the town was hard by, they soon had reached their lodging-place. There they were received with joy. The host with kindness welcomed them, and with joy and gladness made generous provision for their needs.

When the squire had done for them all the honour that he could do, he came and mounted his horse again, leading it off in front of the Count's bower to the stable. The Count and three of his vassals were leaning out of the bower, when the Count, seeing his squire mounted on the dappled steed, asked him whose it was. And he replied that it was his. The Count, greatly astonished, says: "How is that? Where didst thou get him?" "A knight whom I esteem highly gave him to me, sire," says he. "I have conducted him within this town, and he is lodged at a burgher's house. He is a very courteous knight and the handsomest man I ever saw. Even if I had given you my word and oath, I could not half tell you how handsome he is." The Count replies: "I suppose and presume that he is not more handsome than I am." "Upon my word, sire," the sergeant says, "you are very handsome and a gentleman. There is not a knight in this country, a native of this land, whom you do not excel in favour. But I dare maintain concerning this one that he is fairer than you, if he were not beaten black and blue beneath his hauberk, and bruised. In the forest he has been fighting single-handed with eight knights, and leads away their eight horses. And there comes with him a lady so fair that never lady was half so fair as she." When the Count hears this news, the desire takes him to go and see if this is true or false. "I never heard such a thing," says he; "take me now to his lodging-place, for certainly I wish to know if thou dost lie or speak the truth." He replies: "Right gladly, sire. This is the way and the path to follow, for it is not far from here." "I am anxious to see them," says the Count. Then he comes down, and the squire gets off his horse, and makes the Count mount in his place. Then he ran ahead to tell

Erec that the Count was coming to visit him. Erec's lodging was rich indeed—the kind to which he was accustomed. There were many tapers and candles lighted all about. The Count came attended by only three companions. Erec, who was of gracious manners, rose to meet him, and exclaimed: "Welcome, sire!" And the Count returned his salutation. They both sat down side by side upon a soft white couch, where they chat with each other. The Count makes him an offer and urges him to consent to accept from him a guarantee for the payment of his expenses in the town. But Erec does not deign to accept, saying he is well supplied with money, and has no need to accept aught from him. They speak long of many things, but the Count constantly glances about in the other direction, where he caught sight of the lady. Because of her manifest beauty, he fixed all his thought on her. He looked at her as much as he could; he coveted her, and she pleased him so that her beauty filled him with love. Very craftily he asked Erec for permission to speak with her. "Sire," he says "I ask a favour of you, and may it not displease you. As an act of courtesy and as a pleasure, I would fain sit by yonder lady's side. With good intent I came to see you both, and you should see no harm in that. I wish to present to the lady my service in all respects. Know well that for love of you I would do whatever may please her." Erec was not in the least jealous and suspected no evil or treachery. "Sire," says he, "I have no objection. You may sit down and talk with her. Don't think that I have any objection. I give you permission willingly." The lady was seated about two spear-lengths away from him. And the Count took his seat close beside her on a low stool. Prudent and courteous, the lady turned toward him. "Alas," quoth he, "how grieved I am to see you in such humble state! I am sorry and feel great distress. But if you would believe my word, you could have honour and great advantage, and much wealth would accrue to you. Such beauty as yours is entitled to great honour and distinction. I would make you my mistress, if it should please you and be your will; you would be my mistress dear and lady over all my land. When I deign to woo you thus, you ought not to disdain my suit. I know and perceive that your lord does not love and esteem you. If you will remain with me, you would be mated with a worthy lord." "Sire," says Enide, "your proposal is vain. It cannot be. Ah! better that I were yet unborn, or burnt upon a fire of thorns and my ashes scattered abroad than that I should ever in any wise be false to my lord, or conceive any felony or treachery toward him. You have made a great mistake in making such a proposal to me. I shall not agree to it in any wise." The Count's ire began to rise. "You disdain to love me, lady?" says he; "upon my word, you are too proud. Neither for flattery nor for prayer you will do my will? It is surely true that a woman's pride mounts the more one prays and flatters her; but whoever insults and dishonours her will often find her more tractable. I give you my word that if you do not do my will there soon will be some sword-play here. Rightly or wrongly, I will have your lord slain right here before your eyes." "Ah, sire," says Enide, "there is a better way than that you say. You would commit a wicked and treacherous deed if you killed him thus. Calm yourself again, I pray; for I will do your pleasure. You may regard me as all your own, for I am yours and wish to be. I did not speak as I did from pride, but to learn and prove if I could find in you the true love of a sincere heart. But I would not at any price have you commit an act of treason. My lord is not on his guard; and if you should kill him thus, you would do a very ugly deed, and I should have the blame for it. Every one in the land would say that it had been done with my consent. Go and rest until the morrow, when my lord shall be about to rise. Then you can better do him harm without blame and without reproach." With her heart's thoughts her words do not agree. "Sire," says she, "believe me now! Have no anxiety; but send here to-morrow your knights and squires and have me carried away by force. My lord will rush to my defence, for he is proud and bold enough. Either in earnest or in jest, have him seized and treated ill, or strike his head off, if you will. I have led this life now long enough; to tell the truth. I like not the company of this my lord. Rather would I feel your body lying beside me in a bed. And since we have reached this point, of my love you may rest assured." The Count replies: "It is well, my lady! God bless the hour that you were born; in great estate you shall be held." "Sire," says she, "indeed, I believe it. And yet I would fain have your word that you will always hold me dear; I could not believe you otherwise." Glad and merry, the Count replies: "See here, my faith I will pledge to you loyally as a Count, Madame, that I shall do all your behests. Have no further fear of that. All you want you shall always have." Then she took his plighted word; but little she valued or cared for it, except therewith to save her lord. Well she knows how to deceive a fool, when she puts her mind upon it. Better it were to lie to him than that her lord should be cut off. The Count now rose from her side, and commends her to God a hundred times. But of little use to him will be the faith which she has pledged to him. Erec knew nothing at all of this that they were plotting to work his death; but God will be able to lend him aid, and I think He will do so. Now Erec is in great peril, and does not know that he must be on his guard. The Count's intentions are very base in planning to steal away his wife and kill him when he is without defence. In treacherous guise he takes his leave: "To God I commend you," says he, and Erec replies: "And so do I you, sire." Thus they separated. Already a good part of the night was passed. Out of the way, in one of the rooms, two beds were made upon the floor. In one of them Erec lays him down, in the other Enide went to rest. Full of grief and anxiety, she never closed her eyes that night, but remained on watch for her lord's sake; for from what she had seen of the Count, she knew him to be full of wickedness. She knows full well that if he once gets possession of her lord, he will not fail to do him harm. He may be sure of being killed: so for his sake she is in distress. All night she must needs keep her vigil; but before the dawn, if she can bring it about, and if her lord will take her word, they will be ready to depart.

Erec slept all night long securely until daylight. Then Enide realised and suspected that she might hesitate too long. Her heart was tender toward her lord, like a good and loyal lady. Her heart was neither deceitful nor false. So she rises and makes ready, and drew near to her lord to wake him up. "Ah, sire," says she, "I crave your pardon. Rise quickly now, for you are betrayed beyond all doubt, though guiltless and free from any crime. The Count is a proven traitor, and if he can but catch you here, you will never get away without his having cut you in pieces. He hates you because he desires me. But if it please God, who knows all things, you shall be neither slain nor caught. Last evening he would have killed you had I not assured him that I would be his mistress and his wife. You will see him return here soon: he wants to seize me and keep me here and kill you if he can find you." Now Erec learns how loyal his wife is to him. "Lady," says he, "have our horses quickly saddled; then run and call our host, and tell him quickly to come here. Treason has been long abroad." Now the horses are saddled, and the lady summoned the host. Erec has armed and dressed himself, and into his presence came the host. "Sire," said he, "what haste is this, that you are risen at such an hour, before the day and the sun appear?" Erec replies that he has a long road and a full day before him, and therefore he has made ready to set out, having it much upon his mind; and he added: "Sire, you have nor yet handed me any statement of my expenses. You have received me with honour and kindness, and therein great merit redounds to you. Cancel my indebtedness with these seven horses that I brought here with me. Do not disdain them, but keep them for your own. I cannot increase my gift to you by so much as the value of a halter." The burgher was delighted with this gift and bowed low, expressing his thanks and gratitude. Then Erec mounts and takes his leave, and they set out upon their way. As they ride, he frequently warns Enide that if she sees anything she should not be so bold as to speak to him about it. Meanwhile, there entered the house a hundred knights well armed, and very much dismayed they were to find Erec no longer there. Then the Count learned that the lady had deceived him. He discovered the footsteps of the horses, and they all followed the trail, the Count threatening Erec and vowing that, if he can come up with him, nothing can keep him from having his head on the spot. "A curse on him who now hangs back, and does not spur on fast!" quoth he; "he who presents me with the head of the knight whom I hate so bitterly, will have served me to my taste." Then they plunge on at topmost speed, filled with hostility toward him who had never laid eyes on them and had never harmed them by deed or word. They ride ahead until they made him out; at the edge of a forest they catch sight of him before he was hid by the forest trees. Not one of them halted then, but all rushed on in rivalry. Enide hears the clang and noise of their arms and horses, and sees that the valley is full of them. As soon as she saw them, she could not restrain her tongue. "Ah, sire," she cries, "alas, how this Count has attacked you, when he leads against you such a host! Sire, ride faster now, until we be within this wood. I think we can easily distance them, for they are still a long way behind. If you go on at this pace, you can never escape from death, for you are no match for them." Erec replies: "Little esteem you have for me, and lightly you hold my words. It seems I cannot correct you by fair request. But as the Lord have mercy upon me until I escape from here, I swear that you shall pay dearly for this speech of yours; that is, unless my mind should change." Then he straightway turns about, and sees the seneschal drawing near upon a horse both strong and fleet. Before them all he takes his stand at the distance of four cross-bow shots. He had not disposed of his arms, but was thoroughly well equipped. Erec reckons up his opponents' strength, and sees there are fully a hundred of them. Then he who thus is pressing him thinks he had better call a hair. Then they ride to meet each other, and strike upon each other's shield great blows with their sharp and trenchant swords. Erec caused his stout steel sword to pierce his body through and through, so that his shield and hauberk protected him no more than a shred of dark-blue silk. And next the Count comes spurring on, who, as the story tells, was a strong and doughty knight. But the Count in this was ill advised when he came with only shield and lance. He placed such trust in his own prowess that he thought that he needed no other arms. He showed his exceeding boldness by rushing on ahead of all his men more than the space of nine acres. When Erec saw him stand alone, he turned toward him; the Count is not afraid of him, and they come together with clash of arms. First the Count strikes him with such violence upon the breast that he would have lost his stirrups if he had not been well set. He makes the wood of his shield to split so that the

iron of his lance protrudes on the other side. But Erec's hauberk was very
solid and protected him from death without the tear of a single mesh. The
Count was strong and breaks his lance; then Erec strikes him with such force
on his yellow painted shield that he ran more than a yard of his lance through
his abdomen, knocking him senseless from his steed. Then he turned and rode
away without further tarrying on the spot. Straight into the forest he spurs at
full speed. Now Erec is in the woods, and the others paused a while over those
who lay in the middle of the field. Loudly they swear and vow that they will
rather follow after him for two or three days than fail to capture and slaughter
him. The Count, though grievously wounded in the abdomen, hears what
they say. He draws himself up a little and opens his eyes a tiny bit. Now he
realises what an evil deed he had begun to execute. He makes the knights step
back, and says: "My lords, I bid you all, both strong and weak, high and low,
that none of you be so bold as to dare to advance a single step. All of you
return now quickly! I have done a villainous deed, and I repent me of my foul
design. The lady who outwitted me is very honourable, prudent, and
courteous. Her beauty fired me with love for her; because I desired her, I
wished to kill her lord and keep her back with me by force. I well deserved
this woe, and now it has come upon me. How abominably disloyal and
treacherous I was in my madness! Never was there a better knight born of
mother than he. Never shall he receive harm through me if I can in any way
prevent it. I command you all to retrace your steps." Back they go
disconsolate, carrying the lifeless seneschal on the shield reversed. The
Count, whose wound was not mortal, lived on for some time after. Thus was
Erec delivered.

Erec goes off at full speed down a road between two hedgerows—he and his
wife with him. Both putting spurs to their horses, they rode until they came
to a meadow which had been mown. After emerging from the hedged
enclosure they came upon a drawbridge before a high tower, which was all
closed about with a wall and a broad and deep moat. They quickly pass over
the bridge, but had not gone far before the lord of the place espied them from
up in his tower. About this man I can tell you the truth: that he was very
small of stature, but very courageous of heart. When he sees Erec cross the
bridge, he comes down quickly from his tower, and on a great sorrel steed of
his he causes a saddle to be placed, which showed portrayed a golden lion.
Then he orders to be brought his shield, his stiff, straight lance, a sharp
polished sword, his bright shining helmet, his gleaming hauberk, and
triple-woven greaves; for he has seen an armed knight pass before his list
against whom he wishes to strive in arms, or else this stranger will strive

against him until he shall confess defeat. His command was quickly done: behold the horse now led forth; a squire brought him around already bridled and with saddle on. Another fellow brings the arms. The knight passed out through the gate, as quickly as possible, all alone, without companion. Erec is riding along a hill-side, when behold the knight comes tearing down over the top of the hill, mounted upon a powerful steed which tore along at such a pace that he crushed the stones beneath his hoofs finer than a millstone grinds the corn; and bright gleaming sparks flew off in all directions, so that it seemed as if his four feet were all ablaze with fire. Enide heard the noise and commotion, and almost fell from her palfrey, helpless and in a faint. There was no vein in her body in which the blood did not turn, and her face became all pale and white as if she were a corpse. Great is her despair and dismay, for she does not dare to address her lord, who often threatens and chides at her and charges her to hold her peace. She is distracted between two courses to pursue, whether to speak or to hold her peace. She takes counsel with herself, and often she prepares to speak, so that her tongue already moves, but the voice cannot issue forth; for her teeth are clenched with fear, and thus shut up her speech within. Thus she admonishes and reproaches herself, but she closes her mouth and grits her teeth so that her speech cannot issue forth. At strife with herself, she said: "I am sure and certain that I shall incur a grievous loss, if here I lose my lord. Shall I tell him all, then, openly? Not I. Why not? I would not dare, for thus I should enrage my lord. And if my lord's ire is once aroused, he will leave me in this wild place alone, wretched and forlorn. Then I shall be worse off than now. Worse off? What care I? May grief and sorrow always be mine as long as I live, if my lord does not promptly escape from here without being delivered to a violent death. But if I do not quickly inform him, this knight who is spurring hither will have killed him before he is aware; for he seems of very evil intent. I think I have waited too long from fear of his vigorous prohibition. But I will no longer hesitate because of his restraint. I see plainly that my lord is so deep in thought that he forgets himself; so it is fight that I should address him." She spoke to him. He threatens her, but has no desire to do her harm, for he realises and knows full well that she loves him above all else, and he loves her, too, to the utmost. He rides toward the knight, who challenges him to battle, and they meet at the foot of the hill, where they attack and defy each other. Both smite each other with their iron-tipped lances with all their strength. The shields that hang about their necks are not worth two coats of bark: the leather tears, and they split the wood, and they shatter the meshes of the hauberks. Both are pierced to the vitals by the lances, and the horses fall to earth. Now, both the warriors were doughty. Grievously, but not mortally, wounded, they quickly got upon their feet and grasped afresh their lances, which were not broken nor the worse for wear. But they cast them away on the ground, and drawing their swords from the scabbard, they attack each other with great fury. Each wounds and injures the other, for there is no mercy on either side. They deal such blows upon the helmets that gleaming sparks fly out when their swords recoil. They split and splinter the shields; they batter and crush the hauberks. In four places the swords are brought down to the bare flesh, so that they are greatly weakened and exhausted. And if both their swords had lasted long without breaking, they would never have retreated, nor would the battle have come to an end before one of them perforce had died. Enide, who was watching them, was almost beside herself with grief. Whoever could have seen her then, as she showed her great woe by wringing her hands, tearing her hair and shedding tears, could have seen a loyal lady. And any man would have been a vulgar wretch who saw and did not pity her. And the knights still fight, knocking the jewels from the helmets and dealing at each other fearful blows. From the third to the ninth hour the battle continued so fierce that no one could in any wise make out which was to have the better of it. Erec exerts himself and strives; he brought his sword down upon his enemy's helmet, cleaving it to the inner lining of mail and making him stagger; but he stood firmly and did not fall. Then he attacked Erec in turn, and dealt him such a blow upon the covering of his shield that his strong and precious sword broke when he tried to pull it out. When he saw that his sword was broken, in a spite he threw as far away as he could the part that remained in his hand. Now he was afraid and must needs draw back; for any knight that lacks his sword cannot do much execution in battle or assault. Erec pursues him until he begs him, for God's sake, not to kill him. "Mercy, noble knight," he cries, "be not so cruel and harsh toward me. Now that I am left without my sword, you have the strength and the power to take my life or make me your prisoner, for I have no means of defence." Erec replies: "When thou thus dost petition me I fain would hear thee admit outright whether thou art defeated and overcome. Thou shalt not again be touched by me if thou dost surrender at my discretion." The knight was slow to make reply. So, when Erec saw him hesitate, in order to further dismay him, he again attacked him, rushing at him with drawn sword; whereupon, thoroughly terrified, he cried: "Mercy, sire! Regard me as your captive, since it cannot be otherwise." Erec answers: "More than that is necessary. You shall not get off so easily as that. Tell me your station and your name, and I in turn will tell you mine." "Sire," says he, "you are right. I am king of this country. My liegemen are Irishmen, and there is none who does not have to pay me rent. My name is Guivret the Little. I am very rich and powerful; for there is no landholder whose lands touch mine in any direction who ever transgresses my command and who does not do my pleasure. I have no neighbour who does not fear me, however proud and bold he may be. But I greatly desire to be your confidant and friend from this time on." Erec replies: "I, too, can boast that I am a noble man. My name is Erec, son of King Lac. My father is king of Farther Wales, and has many a rich city, fine hall, and strong town; no king or emperor has more than he, save only King Arthur. Him, of course, I except; for with him none can compare." Guivret is greatly astonished at this, and says: "Sire, a great marvel is this I hear. I was never so glad of anything as of your acquaintance. You may put full trust in me! And should it please you to abide in my country within my estates, I shall have you treated with great honour. So long as you care to remain here, you shall be recognised as my lord. We both have need of a physician, and I have a castle of mine near here, not eight leagues away, nor even seven. I wish to take you thither with me, and there we shall have our wounds tended." Erec replies: "I thank you for what I have heard you say. However, I will not go, thank you. But only so much I request of you, that if I should be in need, and you should hear that I had need of aid, you would not then forget me." "Sire" says he, "I promise you that never, so long as I am alive, shall you have need of my help but that I shall go at once to aid you with all the assistance I can command." "I have nothing more to ask of you," says Erec; "you have promised me much. You are now my lord and friend, if your deed is as good as your word." Then each kisses and embraces the other. Never was there such an affectionate parting after such a fierce battle; for from very affection and generosity each one cut off long, wide strips from the bottom of his shirt and bound up the other's wounds. When they had thus bandaged each other, they commended each other to God.

So thus they parted. Guivret takes his way back alone, while Erec resumed his road, in dire need of plaster wherewith to heal his wounds. He did not cease to travel until he came to a plain beside a lofty forest all full of stags, hinds, deer, does, and other beasts, and all sorts of game. Now King Arthur and the Queen and the best of his barons had come there that very day. The King wished to spend three or four days in the forest for pleasure and sport, and had commanded tents, pavilions, and canopies to be brought. My lord Gawain had stepped into the King's tent, all tired out by a long ride. In front of the tent a white beech stood, and there he had left a shield of his, together with his ashen lance. He left his steed, all saddled and bridled, fastened to a branch by the rein. There the horse stood until Kay the seneschal came by.

He came up quickly and, as if to beguile the time, took the steed and mounted, without the interference of any one. He took the lance and the shield, too, which were close by under the tree. Galloping along on the steed, Kay rode along a valley until it came about by chance that Erec met him. Now Erec recognised the seneschal, and he knew the arms and the horse, but Kay did not recognise him, for he could not be distinguished by his arms. So many blows of sword and lance had he received upon his shield that all the painted design had disappeared from it. And the lady, who did not wish to be seen or recognised by him, shrewdly held her veil before her face, as if she were doing it because of the sun's glare and the dust. Kay approached rapidly and straightway seized Erec's rein, without so much as saluting him. Before he let him move, he presumptuously asked him: "Knight," says he, "I wish to know who you are and whence you come." "You must be mad to stop me thus," says Erec; "you shall not know that just now." And the other replies: "Be not angry; I only ask it for your good. I can see and make out clearly that you are wounded and hurt. If you will come along with me you shall have a good lodging this night; I shall see that you are well cared for, honoured and made comfortable: for you are in need of rest. King Arthur and the Queen are close by here in a wood, lodged in pavilions and tents. In all good faith, I advise you to come with me to see the Queen and King, who will take much pleasure in you and will show you great honour." Erec replies: "You say well; yet will I not go thither for anything. You know not what my business is: I must yet farther pursue my way. Now let me go; too long I stay. There is still some daylight left." Kay makes answer: "You speak madness when you decline to come. I trow you will repent of it. And however much it may be against your will, you shall both go, as the priest goes to the council, willy-nilly. To-night you will be badly served, if, unmindful of my advice, you go there as strangers. Come now quickly, for I will take you." At this word Erec's ire was roused. "Vassal," says he, "you are mad to drag me thus after you by force. You have taken me quite off my guard. I tell you you have committed an offence. For I thought to be quite safe, and was not on my guard against you." Then he lays his hand upon his sword and cries: "Hands off my bridle, vassal! Step aside. I consider you proud and impudent. I shall strike you, be sure of that, if you drag me longer after you. Leave me alone now." Then he lets him go, and draws off across the field more than an acre's width; then turns about and, as a man with evil intent, issues his challenge. Each rushed at the other. But, because Kay was without armour, Erec acted courteously and turned the point of his lance about and presented the butt-end instead. Even so, he gave him such a blow high up on the broad expanse of his shield that he caused it to wound him on the temple, pinning his arm to his breast: all prone he throws him to the earth. Then he went to catch the horse and hands him over by the bridle to Enide. He was about to lead it away, when the wounded man with his wonted flattery begs him to restore it courteously to him. With fair words he flatters and wheedles him. "Vassal," says he, "so help me God, that horse is not mine. Rather does it belong to that knight in whom dwells the greatest prowess in the world, my lord Gawain the Bold. I tell you so much on his behalf, in order that you may send it back to him and thus win honour. So shall you be courteous and wise, and I shall be your messenger." Erec makes answer: "Take the horse, vassal, and lead it away. Since it belongs to my lord Gawain it is not meet that I should appropriate it." Kay takes the horse, remounts, and coming to the royal tent, tells the King the whole truth, keeping nothing back. And the King summoned Gawain, saying: "Fair nephew Gawain, if ever you were true and courteous, go quickly after him and ask him in winsome wise who he is and what his business. And if you can influence him and bring him along with you to us, take care not to fail to do so." Then Gawain mounts his steed, two squires following after him. They soon made Erec out, but did not recognise him. Gawain salutes him, and he Gawain: their greetings were mutual. Then said my lord Gawain with his wonted openness: "Sire," says he, "King Arthur sends me along this way to encounter you. The Queen and King send you their greeting, and beg you urgently to come and spend some time with them (it may benefit you and cannot harm), as they are close by." Erec replies: "I am greatly obliged to the King and Queen and to you who are, it seems, both kind of heart and of gentle mien. I am not in a vigorous state; rather do I bear wounds within my body: yet will I not turn aside from my way to seek a lodging-place. So you need not longer wait: I thank you, but you may be gone." Now Gawain was a man of sense. He draws back and whispers in the ear of one of the squires, bidding him go quickly and tell the King to take measures at once to take down and lower his tents and come and set them up in the middle of the road three or four leagues in advance of where they now are. There the King must lodge to-night, if he wishes to meet and extend hospitality to the best knight in truth whom he can ever hope to see; but who will not go out of his way for a lodging at the bidding of any one. The fellow went and gave his message. The King without delay causes his tents to be taken down. Now they are lowered, the sumpters loaded, and off they set. The King mounted Aubagu, and the Queen afterwards mounted a white Norse palfrey. All this while, my lord Gawain did not cease to detain Erec, until the latter said to him: "Yesterday I covered more ground than I shall do to-day. Sire, you annoy me;

let me go. You have already disturbed a good part of my day." And my lord Gawain answers him: "I should like to accompany you a little way, if you do not object; for it is yet a long while until night. They spent so much time in talking that all the tents were set up before them, and Erec sees them, and perceives that his lodging is arranged for him. "Ah! Gawain," he says, "your shrewdness has outwitted me. By your great cunning you have kept me here. Since it has turned out thus, I shall tell you my name at once. Further concealment would be useless. I am Erec, who was formerly your companion and friend." Gawain hears him and straightway embraces him. He raised up his helmet and unlaced his mouthpiece. Joyfully he clasps him in his embrace, while Erec embraces him in turn. Then Gawain leaves him, saying, "Sire, this news will give great pleasure to my lord; he and my lady will both be glad, and I must go before to tell them of it. But first I must embrace and welcome and speak comfortably to my lady Enide, your wife. My lady the Queen has a great desire to see her. I heard her speak of her only yesterday." Then he steps up to Enide and asks her how she is, if she is well and in good case. She makes answer courteously: "Sire, I should have no cause for grief, were I not in great distress for my lord; but as it is, I am in dismay, for he has hardly a limb without a wound." Gawain replies: "This grieves me much. It is perfectly evident from his face, which is all pale and colourless. I could have wept myself when I saw him so pale and wan, but my joy effaced my grief, for at sight of him I felt so glad that I forgot all other pain. Now start and ride along slowly. I shall ride ahead at top-speed to tell the Queen and the King that you are following after me. I am sure that they will both be delighted when they hear it." Then he goes, and comes to the King's tent. "Sire," he cries, "now you and my lady must be glad, for here come Erec and his wife." The King leaps to his feet with joy. "Upon my word!" he says, "right glad I am. I could hear no news which could give me so much happiness." The Queen and all the rest rejoice, and come out from the tents as fast as they may. Even the King comes forth from his pavilion, and they met Erec near at band. When Erec sees the King coming, he quickly dismounts, and Enide too. The King embraces and meets them, and the Queen likewise tenderly kisses and embraces them: there is no one that does not show his joy. Right there, upon the spot, they took off Erec's armour; and when they saw his wounds, their joy turned to sadness. The King draws a deep sigh at the sight of them, and has a plaster brought which Morgan, his sister, had made. This piaster, which Morgan had given to Arthur, was of such sovereign virtue that no wound, whether on nerve or joint, provided it were treated with the piaster once a day, could fail to be completely cured and healed within a week. They brought to the King the piaster which gave Erec great relief. When they had bathed, dried, and bound up his wounds, the King leads him and Enide into his own royal tent, saying that he intends, out of love for Erec, to tarry in the forest a full fortnight, until he be completely restored to health. For this Erec thanks the King, saying: "Fair sire, my wounds are not so painful that I should desire to abandon my journey. No one could detain me; to-morrow, without delay, I shall wish to get off in the morning, as soon as I see the dawn." At this the King shook his head and said: "This is a great mistake for you not to remain with us. I know that you are far from well. Stay here, and you will do the right thing. It will be a great pity and cause for grief if you die in this forest. Fair gentle friend, stay here now until you are quite yourself again." Erec replies: "Enough of this. I have undertaken this journey, and shall not tarry in any wise." The King hears that he would by no means stay for prayer of his; so he says no more about it, and commands the supper to be prepared at once and the tables to be spread. The servants go to make their preparations. It was a Saturday night; so they ate fish and fruit, pike and perch, salmon and trout, and then pears both raw and cooked. Soon after supper they ordered the beds to be made ready. The King, who held Erec dear, had him laid in a bed alone; for he did not wish that any one should lie with him who might touch his wounds. That night he was well lodged. In another bed close by lay Enide with the Queen under a cover of ermine, and they all slept in great repose until the day broke next morning.

Next day, as soon as it is dawn. Erec arises, dresses, commands his horses to be saddled, and orders his arms to be brought to him. The valets run and bring them to him. Again the King and all the knights urge him to remain; but entreaty is of no avail, for he will not stay for anything. Then you might have seen them all weep and show such grief as if they already saw him dead. He puts on his arms, and Enide arises. All the knights are sore distressed, for they think they will never see them more. They follow them out from the tents, and send for their own horses, that they may escort and accompany them. Erec said to them: "Be not angry! but you shall not accompany me a single step. I'll thank you if you'll stay behind!" His horse was brought to him, and he mounts without delay. Taking his shield and lance, he commends them all to God, and they in turn wish Erec well. Then Enide mounts, and they ride away.

Entering a forest, they rode on without halting till hour of prime. While they thus traversed the wood, they heard in the distance the cry of a damsel in great distress. When Erec heard the cry, he felt sure from the sound that it was the voice of one in trouble and in need of help. Straightway calling

Enide, he says: "Lady, there is some maiden who goes through the wood
calling aloud. I take it that she is in need of aid and succour. I am going to
hasten in that direction and see what her trouble is. Do you dismount and
await me here, while I go yonder." "Gladly, sire," she says. Leaving her alone,
he makes his way until he found the damsel, who was going through the
wood, lamenting her lover whom two giants had taken and were leading away
with very cruel treatment. The maiden was rending her garments, and tearing
her hair and her tender crimson face. Erec sees her and, wondering greatly,
begs her to tell him why she cries and weeps so sore. The maiden cries and
sighs again, then sobbing, says: "Fair sire, it is no wonder if I grieve, for I wish
I were dead. I neither love nor prize my life, for my lover has been led away
prisoner by two wicked and cruel giants who are his mortal enemies. God!
what shall I do? Woe is me! deprived of the best knight alive, the most noble
and the most courteous. And now he is in great peril of death. This very day,
and without cause, they will bring him to some vile death. Noble knight, for
God's sake, I beg you to succour my lover, if now you can lend him any aid.
You will not have to run far, for they must still be close by." "Damsel," says
Erec, "I will follow them, since you request it, and rest assured that I shall do
all within my power: either I shall be taken prisoner along with him, or I shall
restore him to you safe and sound. If the giants let him live until I can find
him, I intend to measure my strength with theirs." "Noble knight," the
maiden said, "I shall always be your servant if you restore to me my lover.
Now go in God's name, and make haste, I beseech you." "Which way lies their
path?" "This way, my lord. Here is the path with the footprints." Then Erec
started at a gallop, and told her to await him there. The maid commends him
to the Lord, and prays God very fervently that He should give him force by
His command to discomfit those who intend evil toward her lover.

Erec went off along the trail, spurring his horse in pursuit of the giants. He
followed in pursuit of them until he caught sight of them before they emerged
from the wood; he saw the knight with bare limbs mounted naked on a nag,
his hands and feet bound as if he were arrested for highway robbery. The
giants had no lances, shields or whetted swords; but they both had clubs and
scourges, with which they were beating him so cruelly that already they had
cut the skin on his back to the bone. Down his sides and flanks the blood ran,
so that the nag was all covered with blood down to the belly. Erec came along
alone after them. He was very sad and distressed about the knight whom he
saw them treat so spitefully. Between two woods in an open field he came up
with them, and asks: "My lords," says he, "for what crime do you treat this
man so ill and lead him along like a common thief? You are treating him too

cruelly. You are driving him just as if he had been caught stealing. It is a monstrous insult to strip a knight naked, and then bind him and beat him so shamefully. Hand him over to me, I beg of you with all good-will and courtesy. I have no wish to demand him of you forcibly." "Vassal," they say, "what business is this of yours? You must be mad to make any demand of us. If you do not like it, try and improve matters." Erec replies: "Indeed, I like it not, and you shall not lead him away so easily. Since you have left the matter in my hands, I say whoever can get possession of him let him keep him. Take your positions. I challenge you. You shall not take him any farther before some blows have been dealt." "Vassal," they reply, "you are mad, indeed, to wish to measure your strength with us. If you were four instead of one, you would have no more strength against us than one lamb against two wolves." "I do not know how it will turn out," Erec replies; "if the sky fails and the earth melts, then many a lark will be caught. Many a man boasts loudly who is of little worth. On guard now, for I am going to attack you." The giants were strong and fierce, and held in their clenched hands their big clubs tipped with iron. Erec went at them lance in rest. He fears neither of them, in spite of their menace and their pride, and strikes the foremost of them through the eye so deep into the brain that the blood and brains spurt out at the back of his neck; that one lies dead and his heart stops beating. When the other saw him dead, he had reason to be sorely grieved. Furious, he went to avenge him: with both hands he raised his club on high and thought to strike him squarely upon his unprotected head: but Erec watched the blow, and received it on his shield. Even so, the giant landed such a blow that it quite stunned him, and almost made him fall to earth from his steed. Erec covers himself with his shield and the giant, recovering himself, thinks to strike again quickly upon his head. But Erec had drawn his sword, and attacked him with such fierceness that the giant was severely handled: he strikes him so hard upon the neck that he splits him down to the saddle-bow. He scatters his bowels upon the earth, and the body falls full length, split in two halves. The knight weeps with joy and, worshipping, praises God who has sent him this aid. Then Erec unbound him, made him dress and arm himself, and mount one of the horses; the other he made him lead with his right hand, and asks him who he is. And he replied: "Noble knight, thou art my liege lord. I wish to regard thee as my lord, as by right I ought to do, for thou hast saved my life, which but now would have been cut off from my body with great torment and cruelty. What chance, fair gentle sire, in God's name, guided thee hither to me, to free me by thy courage from the hands of my enemies? Sire, I wish to do thee homage. Henceforth, I shall always accompany thee and serve thee as my lord." Erec sees that he is disposed to serve him gladly, if he may, and says: "Friend, for your service I have no desire; but you must know that I came hither to succour you at the instance of your lady, whom I found sorrowing in this wood. Because of you, she grieves and moans; for full of sorrow is her heart. I wish to present you to her now. As soon as I have reunited you with her, I shall continue my way alone; for you have no call to go with me. I have no need cf your company; but I fain would know your name." "Sire," says he, "as you wish. Since you desire to know my name, it must not be kept from you. My name is Cadoc of Tabriol: know that thus I am called. But since I must part from you. I should like to know, if it may be, who you are and of what land, where I may sometime find and search for you, when I shall go a way from here." Erec replies: "Friend, that I will never confide to you. Never speak of it again; but if you wish to find it out and do me honour in any wise go quickly now without delay to my lord, King Arthur, who with might and main is hunting the stag in yonder wood, as I take it, not five short leagues from here. Go thither quickly and take him word that you are sent to him as a gift by him whom yesterday within his tent he joyfully received and lodged. And be careful not to conceal from him from what peril I set free both your life and body. I am dearly cherished at the court, and if you present yourself in my name you will do me a service and honour. There you shall ask who I am; but you cannot know it otherwise." "Sire," says Cadoc, "I will follow your bidding in all respects. You need never have any fear that I do not go with a glad heart. I shall tell the King the full truth regarding the battle which you have fought on my behalf." Thus speaking, they continued their way until they came to the maiden where Erec had left her. The damsel's joy knew no bounds when she saw coming her lover whom she never thought to see again. Taking him by the hand, Erec presents him to her with the words: "Grieve no longer, demoiselle! Behold your lover glad and joyous." And she with prudence makes reply: "Sire, by right you have won us both. Yours we should be, to serve and honour. But who could ever repay half the debt we owe you?" Erec makes answer: "My gentle lady, no recompense do I ask of you. To God I now commend you both, for too long, methinks, I have tarried here." Then he turns his horse about, and rides away as fast as he can. Cadoc of Tabriol with his damsel rides off in another direction; and soon he told the news to King Arthur and the Queen.

Erec continues to ride at great speed to the place where Enide was awaiting him in great concern, thinking that surely he had completely deserted her. And he, too, was in great fear lest some one, finding her alone, might have carried her off. So he made all haste to return. But the heat of the day was such, and his arms caused him such distress, that his wounds broke open and burst the bandages. His wounds never stopped bleeding before he came directly to the spot where Enide was waiting for him. She espied him and rejoiced: but she did not realise or know the pain from which he was suffering; for all his body was bathed in blood, and his heart hardly had strength to beat. As he was descending a hill he fell suddenly over upon his horse's neck. As he tried to straighten up, he lost his saddle and stirrups, falling, as if lifeless, in a faint. Then began such heavy grief, when Enide saw him fall to earth. Full of fear at the sight of him, she runs toward him like one who makes no concealment of her grief. Aloud she cries, and wrings her hands: not a shred of her robe remains untorn across her breast. She begins to tear her hair and lacerate her tender face. "Ah God!" she cries, "fair gentle Lord, why dost Thou let me thus live on? Come Death, and kill me hastily!" With these words she faints upon his body. When she recovered, she said to herself reproachfully: "Woe is me, wretched Enide; I am the murderer of my lord, in having killed him by my speech. My lord would still be now alive, if I in my mad presumption had not spoken the word which engaged him in this adventure. Silence never harmed any one, but speech often worketh woe. The truth of this I have tried and proved in more ways than one." Beside her lord she took her seat, holding his head upon her lap. Then she begins her dole anew. "Alas," she says, "my lord, unhappy thou, thou who never hadst a peer; for in thee was beauty seen and prowess was made manifest; wisdom had given thee its heart, and largess set a crown upon thee, without which no one is esteemed. But what did I say? A grievous mistake I made in uttering the word which has killed my lord—that fatal poisoned word for which I must justly be reproached; and I recognise and admit that no one is guilty but myself; I alone must be blamed for this." Then fainting she falls upon the ground, and when she later sat up again, she only moans again the more: "God, what shall I do, and why live on? Why does Death delay and hesitate to come and seize me without respite? Truly, Death holds me in great contempt! Since Death does not deign to take my life, I must myself perforce achieve the vengeance for my sinful deed. Thus shall I die in spite of Death, who will not heed my call for aid. Yet, I cannot die through mere desire, nor would complaining avail me aught. The sword, which my lord had gilded on, ought by right to avenge his death. I will not longer consume myself in distress, in prayer, and vain desire." She draws the sword forth from its sheath and begins to consider it. God, who is full of mercy, caused her to delay a little; and while she passes in review her sorrow and her misfortune, behold there comes riding apace a Count with numerous suite, who from afar had heard the lady's loud outcry. God did not wish to desert her; for now she would have killed herself, had she not been surprised by those who took away from her the sword and thrust it back into its sheath. The Count then dismounted from his horse and began to inquire of her concerning the knight, and whether she was his wife or his lady-love. "Both one and the other, sire," she says, "my sorrow is such as I cannot tell. Woe is me that I am not dead." And the Count begins to comfort her: "Lady," he says, "by the Lord, I pray you, to take some pity on yourself! It is meet that you should mourn, but it is no use to be disconsolate; for you may yet rise to high estate. Do not sink into apathy, but comfort yourself; that will be wise, and God will give you joy again. Your wondrous beauty holds good fortune in store for you; for I will take you as my wife, and make you a countess and dame of rank: this ought to bring you much consolation. And I shall have the body removed and laid away with great honour. Leave off now this grief of yours which in your frenzy you display." And she replies: "Sire, begone! For God's sake, let me be! You can accomplish nothing here. Nothing that one could say or do could ever make me glad again." At this the Count drew back and said: "Let us make a bier, whereon to carry away this body with the lady to the town of Limors. There the body shall be interred. Then will I espouse the lady, whether or not she give consent: for never did I see any one so fair, nor desire any as I do her. Happy I am to have met with her. Now make quickly and without delay a proper bier for this dead knight. Halt not for the trouble, nor from sloth." Then some of his men draw out their swords and soon cut two saplings, upon which they laid branches cross-wise. Upon this litter they laid Erec down; then hitched two horses to it. Enide rides alongside, not ceasing to make lament, and often fainting and falling back; but the horsemen hold her tight, and try to support her with their arms, and raise her up and comfort her. All the way to Limors they escort the body, until they come to the palace of the Count. All the people follow up after them—ladies, knights, and townspeople. In the middle off the hall upon a dais they stretched the body out full length, with his lance and shield alongside. The hall is full, the crowd is dense. Each one is anxious to inquire what is this trouble, what marvel here. Meanwhile the Count takes counsel with his barons privily. "My lords," he says, "upon the spot I wish to espouse this lady here. We can plainly judge by her beauty and prudent mien that she is of very gentle rank. Her beauty and noble bearing show that the honour of a kingdom or empire might well be bestowed upon her. I shall never suffer disgrace through her; rather I think to win more honour. Have my chaplain summoned now, and do you go and fetch the lady. The half of all my land I will give her as her dower if she will comply with my desire." Then they bade the chaplain come, in accordance with the Count's command, and the dame they brought there, too, and made her marry him perforce; for she flatly refused to give consent. But in spite of all, the Count married her in accordance with his wish. And when he had married her, the constable at once had the tables set in the palace, and had the food prepared; for already it was time for the evening meal.

After vespers, that day in May, Enide was in sore distress, nor did her grief cease to trouble her. And the Count urged her mildly by prayer and threat to make her peace and be consoled, and he made her sit down upon a chair, though it was against her will. In spite of her, they made her take a seat and placed the table in front of her. The Count takes his place on the other side, almost beside himself with rage to find that he cannot comfort her. "Lady," he says, "you must now leave off this grief and banish it. You can have full trust in me, that honour and riches will be yours. You must surely realise that mourning will not revive the dead; for no one ever saw such a thing come about. Remember now, though poor you were, that great riches are within your reach. Once you were poor; rich now you will be. Fortune has not been stingy toward you, in bestowing upon you the honour of being henceforth hailed as Countess. It is true that your lord is dead. If you grieve and lament because of this, do you think that I am surprised? Nay. But I am giving you the best advice I know how to give. In that I have married you, you ought to be content. Take care you do not anger me! Eat now, as I bid you do." And she replies: "Not I, my lord. In faith, as long as I live I will neither eat nor drink unless I first see my lord eat who is lying on yonder dais" "Lady, that can never be. People will think that you are mad when you talk such great nonsense. You will receive a poor reward if you give occasion to-day for further reproof." To this she vouchsafed no reply, holding his threats in slight esteem, and the Count strikes her upon the face. At this she shrieks, and the barons present blame the Count. "Hold, sire!" they cry to the Count; "you ought to be ashamed of having struck this lady because she will not eat. You have done a very ugly deed. If this lady is distressed because of her lord whom she now sees dead, no one should say that she is wrong." "Keep silence, all." the Count replies; "the dame is mine and I am hers, and I will do with her as I please." At this she could not hold her peace, but swears she will never be his. And the Count springs up and strikes her again, and she cries out aloud. "Ha! wretch," she says, "I care not what thou say to me, or what thou do! I fear not thy blows, nor yet thy threats. Beat me and strike me, as thou wilt. I shall never heed thy power so much as to do thy bidding more or less, even were thou with thy hands fight now to snatch out my eyes or flay me alive."

In the midst of these words and disputes Erec recovered from his swoon, like a man who awakes from sleep. No wonder that he was amazed at the crowd of people he saw around. But great was his grief and great his woe when he heard the voice of his wife. He stepped to the floor from off the dais and quickly drew his sword. Wrath and the love he bore his wife gave him courage. He runs thither where he sees her, and strikes the Count squarely upon the head, so that he beats out his brains and, knocking in his forehead, leaves him senseless and speechless; his blood and brains flow out. The knights spring from the tables, persuaded that it is the devil who had made his way among them there. Of young or old there none remains, for all were thrown in great dismay. Each one tries to outrun the other in beating a hasty retreat. Soon they were all clear of the palace, and cry aloud, both weak and strong: "Flee, flee, here comes the corpse!" At the door the press is great: each one strives to make his escape, and pushes and shoves as best he may. He who is last in the surging throng would fain get into the foremost line. Thus they make good their escape in flight, for one dares not stand upon another's going. Erec ran to seize his shield, hanging it about his neck by the strap, while Enide lays hands upon the lance. Then they step out into the courtyard. There is no one so bold as to offer resistance; for they did not believe it could be a man who had thus expelled them, but a devil or some enemy who had entered the dead body. Erec pursues them as they flee, and finds outside in the castle-yard a stable-boy in the act of leading his steed to the watering-place, all equipped with bridle and saddle. This chance encounter pleased Erec well: as he steps up quickly to the horse, the boy in fear straightway yields him up. Erec takes his seat between the saddle-bows, while Enide, seizing the stirrup, springs up on to the horse's neck, as Erec, who bade her mount, commanded and instructed her to do. The horse bears them both away; and finding open the town gate, they make their escape without detention. In the town there was great anxiety about the Count who had been killed; but there is no one, however brave, who follows Erec to take revenge. At his table the Count was slain; while Erec, who bears his wife away, embraces and kisses and gives her cheer. In his arms he clasps her against his heart, and says: "Sweet sister mine, my proof of you has been complete! Be no more concerned in any wise, for I love you now more than ever I did before; and I am certain and rest assured that you love me with a perfect love. From this time on for evermore, I offer myself to do your will just as I used to do before. And if you have spoken ill of me, I pardon you and call you quit of both the offence and the word you spoke." Then he kisses her again and clasps her tight. Now Enide is not ill at ease when her lord clasps and kisses her and tells her again that he loves her still. Rapidly through the night they ride, and they are very glad that the moon shines bright.

Meanwhile, the news has travelled fast, and there is nothing else so quick. The news had reached Guivret the Little that a knight wounded with arms had been found dead in the forest, and that with him was a lady making moan, and so wondrous fair that Iseut would have seemed her waiting-maid. Count Oringle of Limors had found them both, and had caused the corpse to be borne away, and wished himself to espouse the lady; but she refused him. When Guivret heard this news, he was by no means pleased; for at once the thought of Erec occurred to him. It came into his heart and mind to go and seek out the lady, and to have the body honourably interred, if it should turn out to be he. He assembled a thousand men-at-arms and knights to take the town. If the Count would not surrender of his own accord the body and the lady, he would put all to fire and flame. In the moonlight shining clear he led his men on toward Limors, with helmets laced, in hauberks clad, and from their necks the shields were hung. Thus, under arms, they all advanced until nearly midnight, when Erec espied them. Now he expects to be ensnared or killed or captured inevitably. He makes Enide dismount beside a thicket-hedge. No wonder if he is dismayed. "Lady, do you stay here," he says, "beside this thicket-hedge a while, until these people shall have passed. I do not wish them to catch sight of you, for I do not know what manner of people they are, nor of what they go in search. I trust we may not attract their attention. But I see nowhere any place where we could take refuge, should they wish to injure us. I know not if any harm may come to me, but not from fear shall I fail to sally out against them. And if any one assails me, I shall not fail to joust with him. Yet, I am so sore and weary that it is no wonder if I grieve. Now to meet them I must go, and do you stay quiet here. Take care that no one see you, until they shall have left you far behind." Behold now Guivret, with lance outstretched, who espied him from afar. They did not recognise each other, for the moon had gone behind the shadow of a dark cloud. Erec was weak and exhausted, and his antagonist was quite recovered from his wounds and blows. Now Erec will be far from wise if he does not promptly make himself known. He steps out from the hedge. And Guivret spurs toward him without speaking to him at all, nor does Erec utter a word to him: he thought he could do more than he could. Whoever tries to run farther than he is able must perforce give up or take a rest. They clash against each other; but the fight was unequal, for one was weak and the other strong. Guivret strikes him with such force that he carries him down to earth from his horse's back. Enide, who was in hiding, when she sees her lord on the ground, expects to be killed and badly used. Springing forth from the hedge, she runs to help her lord. If she grieved before, now her anguish is greater. Coming up to Guivret, she seized his horse's rein, and then said: "Cursed be thou, knight! For thou hast attacked a weak and exhausted man, who is in pain and mortally wounded, with such injustice that thou canst not find reason for thy deed. If thou hadst been alone and helpless, thou wouldst have rued this attack, provided my lord had been in health. Now be generous and courteous, and kindly let cease this battle which thou hast begun. For thy reputation would be no better for having killed or captured a knight who has not the strength to rise, as thou canst see. For he has suffered so many blows of arms that he is all covered with wounds" And he replies: "Fear not, lady! I see that loyally you love your lord, and I commend you for it. Have no fear whatsoever of me or of my company. But tell me now without concealment what is the name of your lord; for only advantage will you get from telling me. Whoever he be, tell me his name; then he shall go safe and unmolested. Neither he nor you have aught to fear, for you are both in safe hands."

Then Enide learns that she is safe, she answers him briefly in a word: "His name is Erec; I ought not to lie, for I see you are honest and of good intent." Guivret, in his delight, dismounts and goes to fall at Erec's feet, where he was lying on the ground. "My lord," he says, "I was going to seek for you, and was on my way to Limors, where I expected to find you dead. It was told and recounted to me as true that Count Oringle had carried off to Limors a knight who was mortally wounded, and that he wickedly intended to marry a lady whom he had found in his company; but that she would have nothing to do with him. And I was coming urgently to aid and deliver her. If he refused to hand over to me both the lady and you without resistance, I should esteem myself of little worth if I left him a foot of earth to stand upon. Be sure that had I not loved you dearly I should never have taken this upon myself. I am Guivret, your friend; but if I have done you any hurt through my failure to recognise you, you surely ought to pardon me." At this Erec sat up, for he could do no more, and said: "Rise up, my friend. Be absolved of the harm you have done me, since you did not recognise me." Guivret gets up, and Erec tells him how he has killed the Count while he sat at meat, and how he had gained possession again of his steed in front of the stable, and how the sergeants and the squires had fled across the yard, crying: "Flee, flee, the corpse is chasing us;" then, how he came near being caught, and how he escaped through the town and down the hill, carrying his wife on his horse's neck: all this adventure of his he told him. Then Guivret said, "Sire, I have a castle here close by, which is well placed in a healthful site. For your comfort and benefit

I wish to take you there to-morrow and have your wounds cared for. I have two charming and sprightly sisters who are skilful in the care of wounds: they will soon completely cure you. To-night we shall let our company lodge here in the fields until morning; for I think a little rest to-night will do you much good. My advice is that we spend the night here." Erec replies: "I am in favour of doing so." So there they stayed and spent the night. They were not reluctant to prepare a lodging-place, but they found few accommodations, for the company was quite numerous. They lodge as best they may among the bushes: Guivret had his tent set up, and ordered tinder to be kindled, that they might have light and cheer. He has tapers taken out from the boxes, and they light them within the tent. Now Enide no longer grieves, for all has turned out well. She strips her lord of his arms and clothes, and having washed his wounds, she dried them and bound them up again; for she would let no one else touch him. Now Erec knows no further reason to reproach her, for he has tried her well and found that she bears great love to him. And Guivret, who treats them kindly, had a high, long bed constructed of quilted coverlids, laid upon grass and reed, which they found in abundance. There they laid Erec and covered him up. Then Guivret opened a box and took out two patties. "Friend," says he, "now try a little of these cold patties, and drink some wine mixed with water. I have as much as six barrels of it, but undiluted it is not good for you; for you are injured and covered with wounds. Fair sweet friend, now try to eat; for it will do you good. And my lady will eat some too—your wife who has been to-day in sore distress on your account. But you have received full satisfaction for all that, and have escaped. So eat now, and I will eat too, fair friend." Then Guivret sat down by Erec's side, and so did Enide who was much pleased by all that Guivret did. Both of them urge him to eat, giving him wine mixed with water'; for unmixed it is too strong and heating. Erec ate as a sick man eats, and drank a little—all he dared. But he rested comfortably and slept all night; for on his account no noise or disturbance was made.

In the early morning they awoke, and prepared again to mount and ride. Erec was so devoted to his own horse that he would ride no other. They gave to Enide a mule, for she had lost her palfrey. But she was not concerned; to judge by her looks, she gave the matter no thought. She had a good mule with an easy gait that bore her very comfortably. And it gave her great satisfaction that Erec was not cast down, but rather assured them that he would recover completely. Before the third hour they reached Penevric, a strong castle, well and handsomely situated. There dwelt the two sisters of Guivret; for the place was agreeable enough. Guivret escorted Erec to a delightful, airy room in a remote part of the castle. His sisters, at his request, exerted themselves to cure Erec; and Erec placed himself in their hands, for they inspired him with perfect confidence. First, they removed the dead flesh, then applied plaster and lint, devoting to his care all their skill, like women who knew their business well. Again and again they washed his wounds and applied the plaster. Four times or more each day they made him eat and drink, allowing him, however, no garlic or pepper. But whoever might go in or out Enide was always with him, being more than any one else concerned. Guivret often came in to ask and inquire if he wanted anything. He was well kept and well served, and everything that he wished was willingly done. But the damsels cheerfully and gladly showed such devotion in caring for him that by the end of a fortnight he felt no hurt or pain. Then, to bring his colour back, they began to give him baths. There was no need to instruct the damsels, for they understood the treatment well. When he was able to walk about. Guivret had two loose gowns made of two different kinds of silk, one trimmed with ermine, the other with vair. One was of a dark purple colour, and the other striped, sent to him as a present by a cousin of his from Scotland. Enide had the purple gown trimmed with ermine, which was very precious, while Erec had the striped stuff with the fur, which was no less valuable. Now Erec was strong and well, cured and recovered. Now that Enide was very happy and had everything she desired, her great beauty returned to her; for her great distress had affected her so much that she was very pale and wan. Now she was embraced and kissed, now she was blessed with all good things, now she had her joy and pleasures; for unadorned they lie in bed and each enfolds and kisses the other; nothing gives them so much joy. They have had so much pain and sorrow, he for her, and she for him, that now they have their satisfaction. Each vies in seeking to please the other. Of their further sport I must not speak. Now they have so welded their love and forgotten their grief that they scarcely remember it any more. But now they must go on their way; so they asked his leave to depart from Guivret, in whom they had found a friend indeed; for he had honoured and served them in every way. When he came to take leave, Erec said: "Sire, I do not wish to delay longer my departure for my own land. Order everything to be prepared and collected, in order that I may have all I need. I shall wish to start to-morrow morning, as soon as it is day. I have stayed so long with you that I feel strong and vigorous. God grant, if it please Him, that I may live to meet you again somewhere, when I may be able in my turn to serve and honour you. Unless I am captured or detained, I do not expect to tarry anywhere until I reach the court of King Arthur, whom I hope to find either at Robais or Carduel." To which Guivret makes prompt reply, "Sire, you shall not go off alone! For I myself shall go with you and shall take companions with us, if it be your pleasure." Erec accedes to this advice, and says that, in accordance with his plans, he wishes the journey to be begun. That night they make preparations for their journey, not wishing to delay there longer. They all make ready and prepare. In the early morning, when they awake, the saddles are placed upon the steeds. Before he leaves, Erec goes to bid farewell to the damsels in their rooms; and Enide (who was glad and full of joy) thither follows him. When their preparations for departure were made, they took their leave of the damsels. Erec, who was very courteous, in taking leave of them, thanks them for his health and life, and pledges to them his service. Then he took one of them by the hand she who was the nearer to him and Enide took the other's hand: hand in hand they came up from the bedroom into the castle hall. Guivret urges them to mount at once without delay. Enide thinks the time will never come for them to mount. They bring around to the block for her a good-tempered palfrey, a soft stepper, handsome and well shaped. The palfrey was of fine appearance and a good mount: it was no less valuable than her own which had stayed behind at Limors. That other one was dappled, this one was sorrel; but the head was of another colour: it was marked in such a way that one cheek was all white, while the other was raven black. Between the two colours there was a line, greener than a grape-vine leaf, which separated the white from the black. Of the bridle, breast-strap, and saddle I can surely say that the workmanship was rich and handsome. All the breast-strap and bridle was of gold set with emeralds. The saddle was decorated in another style, covered with a precious purple cloth. The saddle-bows were of ivory, on which was carved the story of how Aeneas came from Troy, how at Carthage with great joy Dido received him to her bed, how Aeneas deceived her, and how for him she killed herself, how Aeneas conquered Laurentum and all Lombardy, of which he was king all his life. Cunning was the workmanship and well carved, all decorated with fine gold. A skilful craftsman, who made it spent more than seven years in carving it, without touching any other piece of work. I do not know whether he sold it; but he ought to have obtained a good price for it. Now that Enide was presented with this palfrey, she was well compensated for the loss of her own. The palfrey, thus richly apparelled, was given to her and she mounted it gladly; then the gentlemen and squires quickly mounted too. For their pleasure and sport Guivret caused to be taken with them rich falcons, both young and moulted, many a tercel and sparrow-hawk, and many a setter and greyhound.

They rode straight on from morn till eve more than thirty Welsh leagues, and then came to the towers of a stronghold, rich and fair, girt all about with a new wall. And all around, beneath this wall, ran a very deep stream, roaring rushing like a storm. Erec stops to look at it, and ask and find out if any one could truly tell him who was the lord of this town. "Friend," said he to his kind companion, "could you tell me the name of this town, and whose it is? Tell me if it belongs to a count or a king. Since you have brought me here, tell me, if you know." "Sire," he says, "I know very well, and will tell you the truth about it. The name of the town is Brandigant, and it is so strong and fine that it fears neither king nor emperor. If France, and all of England, and all who live from here to Liege were ranged about to lay a siege, they would never take it in their lives; for the isle on which the town stands stretches away four leagues or more, and within the enclosure grows all that a rich town needs: fruit and wheat and wine are found; and of wood and water there is no lack. It fears no assault on any side, nor could anything reduce it to starvation. King Evrain had it fortified, and he has possessed it all his days unmolested, and will possess it all his life. But not because he feared any one did he thus fortify it; but the town is more pleasing so. For if it had no wall or tower, but only the stream that encircles it, it would still be so secure and strong that it would have no fear of the whole world." "God!" said Erec, "what great wealth! Let us go and see the fortress, and we shall take lodging in the town, for I wish to stop here." "Sire," said the other in great distress, "were it not to disappoint you, we should not stop here. In the town there is a dangerous passage." "Dangerous?" says Erec; "do you know about it? Whatever it be, tell us about it; for very gladly would I know." "Sire," says he, "I should fear that you might suffer some harm there. I know there is so much boldness and excellence in your heart that, were I to tell you what I know of the perilous and hard adventure, you would wish to enter in. I have often heard the story, and more than seven years have passed since any one that went in quest of the adventure has come back from the town; yet, proud, bold knights have come hither from many a land. Sire, do not treat this as a jest: for you will never learn the secret from me until you shall have promised me, by the love you have sworn to me, that never by you will be undertaken this adventure, from which no one escapes without receiving shame or death."

Now Erec hears what pleases him, and begs Guivret not to be grieved, saying: "Ah, fair sweet friend, permit that our lodging be made in the town, and do not be disturbed. It is time to halt for the night, and so I trust that it will not displease you; for if any honour comes to us here you ought to be very glad. I appeal to you conceding the adventure that you tell me just the name of it, and I'll not insist upon the rest." "Sire." he says, "I cannot be silent and refuse the information you desire. The name is very fair to say, but the execution is very hard: for no one can come from it alive. The adventure, upon my word, is called 'the Joy of the Court.'" "God! there can be nothing but good in joy," says Erec; "I go to seek it. Don't go now and discourage me about this or anything else, fair gentle friend; but let us have our lodgings taken, for great good may come to us of this. Nothing could restrain me from going to seek the Joy." "Sire," says he, "God grant your prayer, that you may find joy and return without mishap. I clearly see that we must go in. Since otherwise it may not be, let us go in. Our lodging is secured; for no knight of high degree, as I have heard it said and told, can enter this castle with intent to lodge here but that King Evrain offers to shelter him. So gentle and courteous is the King that he has given notice to all his townsmen, appealing to their love for him, that any gentleman from afar should not find lodging in their houses, so that he himself may do honour to all gentlemen who may wish to tarry here."

Thus they proceed toward the castle, passing the list and the drawbridge; and when they passed the listing-place, the people who were gathered in the streets in crowds see Erec in all his beauty, and apparently they think and believe that all the others are in his train. Marvelling much, they stare at him; the whole town was stirred and moved, as they take counsel and discuss about him. Even the maidens at their song leave off their singing and desist, as all together they look at him; and because of his great beauty they cross themselves, and marvellously they pity him. One to another whispers low: "Alas! This knight, who is passing, is on his way to the 'Joy of the Court.' He will be sorry before he returns; no one ever came from another land to claim the 'Joy of the Court' who did not receive shame and harm, and leave his head there as a forfeit." Then, that he may hear their words, they cry-aloud: "God defend thee, knight, from harm; for thou art wondrously handsome, and thy beauty is greatly to be pitied, for to-morrow we shall see it quenched. Tomorrow thy death is come; to-morrow thou shalt surely die if God does not guard and defend thee." Erec hears and understands that they are speaking of him through the lower town: more than two thousand pitied him; but nothing causes him dismay. He passes on without delay, bowing gaily to men and women alike. And they all salute him too; and most of them swear with anxiety, fearing more than he does himself, for his shame and for his hurt. The mere sight of his countenance, his great beauty and his bearing, has so won to him the hearts of all, that knights, ladies, and maids alike fear his harm. King Evrain hears the news that men were arriving at his court who brought with them a numerous train, and by his harness it appeared that their leader was a count or king. King Evrain comes down the street to meet them, and saluting them he cries: "Welcome to this company, both to the master and all his suite. Welcome, gentlemen! Dismount." They dismounted, and there were plenty to receive and take their horses. Nor was King Evrain backward when he saw Enide coming; but he straightway saluted her and ran to help her to dismount. Taking her white and tender hand, he led her up into the palace, as was required by courtesy, and honoured her in every way he could, for he knew right well what he ought to do, without nonsense and without malice. He ordered a chamber to be scented with incense, myrrh, and aloes. When they entered, they all complimented King Evrain on its fine appearance. Hand in hand they enter the room, the King escorting them and taking great pleasure in them. But why should I describe to you the paintings and the silken draperies with which the room was decorated? I should only waste time in folly, and I do not wish to waste it, but rather to hasten on a little; for he who travels the straight road passes him who turns aside; therefore I do not wish to tarry. When the time and hour arrived, the King orders supper to be prepared; but I do not wish to stop over that if I can find some more direct way. That night they had in abundance all that heart desires and craves: birds, venison, and fruit, and wines of different sorts. But better than all is a happy cheer! For of all dishes the sweetest is a joyful countenance and a happy face. They were very richly served until Erec suddenly left off eating and drinking, and began speaking of what rested most upon his heart: he remembered 'the Joy', and began a conversation about it in which King Evrain joined. "Sire" says he, "it is time now to tell you what I intend, and why I have come here. Too long I have refrained from speech, and now can no longer conceal my object. I ask you for 'the Joy' of the Court, for I covet nothing else so much. Grant it to me, whatever it be, if you are in control of it." "In truth, fair friend." the King replies, "I hear you speak great nonsense. This is a very parlous thing, which has caused sorrow to many a worthy man; you yourself will eventually be killed and undone if you will not heed my counsel. But if you were willing to take my word, I should advise you to desist from soliciting so grievous a thing in which you would never succeed. Speak of it no more! Hold your peace! It would be imprudent on your part not to follow my advice. I am not at all surprised that you desire honour and fame; but if I should see you harmed or injured in your body I should be distressed at heart. And know well that I have seen many a man ruined who solicited this joy. They were never any the better for it, but rather did they all die and perish. Before to-morrow's evening come you may expect a like reward. If you wish to strive for the Joy, you shall do so, though it grieve me sore. It is something from which you are free to retreat and draw back if you wish to work your welfare. Therefore I tell you, for I should commit treachery and do you wrong were I not to tell you all the truth." Erec hears him and admits that the King with reason counsels him. But the greater the wonder and the more perilous the adventure, the more he covets it and yearns for it, saying: "Sire, I can tell you that I find you a worthy and a loyal man, and I can put no blame on you. I wish to undertake this boon, however it may fall out with me. The die is cast, for I shall never draw back from anything I have undertaken without exerting all my strength before I quit the field." "I know that well," the King replied; "you are acting against my will. You shall have the Joy which you desire. But I am in great despair; for I greatly fear you will be undone. But now be assured that you shall have what you desire. If you come out of it happily, you will have won such great honour that never did man win greater; and may God, as I desire, grant you a joyous deliverance."

All that night they talked of it, until the beds were prepared and they went to rest. In the morning, when it was daylight, Erec, who was on the watch, saw the clear dawn and the sun, and quickly rising, clothed himself. Enide again is in distress, very sad and ill at ease; all night she is greatly disquieted with the solicitude and fear which she felt for her lord, who is about to expose himself to great peril. But nevertheless he equips himself, for no one can make him change his mind. For his equipment the King sent him, when he arose, arms which he put to good use. Erec did not refuse them, for his own were worn and impaired and in bad state. He gladly accepted the arms and had himself equipped with them in the hall. When he was armed, he descends the steps and finds his horse saddled and the King who had mounted. Every one in the castle and in the houses of the town hastened to mount. In all the town there remained neither man nor woman, erect or deformed, great or small, weak or strong, who is able to go and does not do so. When they start, there is a great noise and clamour in all the streets; for those of high and low degree alike cry out: "Alas, alas! oh knight, the Joy that thou wishest to win has betrayed thee, and thou goest to win but grief and death." And there is not one but says: "God curse this joy! which has been the death of so many gentlemen. To-day it will wreak the worst woe that it has ever yet wrought." Erec hears well and notes that up and down they said of him: "Alas, alas, ill-starred wert thou, fair, gentle, skilful knight! Surely it would not be just that thy life should end so soon, or that harm should come to wound and injure thee." He hears clearly the words and what they said; but notwithstanding, he passes on without lowering his head, and without the bearing of a craven. Whoever may speak, he longs to see and know and understand why they are all in such distress, anxiety, and woe. The King leads him without the town into a garden that stood near by; and all the people follow after, praying that from this trial God may grant him a happy issue. But it is not meet that I should pass on, from weariness and exhaustion of tongue, without telling you the whole truth about the garden, according as the story runs.

The garden had around it no wall or fence except of air: yet, by a spell, the garden was on all sides so shut in by the air that nothing could enter there any more than if the garden were enclosed in iron, unless it flew in over the top. And all through the summer and the winter, too, there were flowers and ripe fruits there; and the fruit was of such a nature that it could be eaten inside; the danger consisted in carrying it out; for whoever should wish to carry out a little would never be able to find the gate, and never could issue from the garden until he had restored the fruit to its place. And there is no flying bird under heaven, pleasing to man, but it sings there to delight and to gladden him, and can be heard there in numbers of every kind. And the earth, however far it stretch, bears no spice or root of use in making medicine, but it had been planted there, and was to be found in abundance. Through a narrow entrance the people entered—King Evrain and all the rest. Erec went riding, lance in rest, into the middle of the garden, greatly delighting in the song of the birds which were singing there; they put him in mind of his Joy the thing he most was longing for. But he saw a wondrous thing, which might arouse fear in the bravest warrior of all whom we know, be it Thiebaut the Esclavon, or Ospinel, or Fernagu. For before them, on sharpened stakes, there stood bright and shining helmets, and each one had beneath the rim a man's head. But at the end there stood a stake where as yet there was nothing but a horn. He knows not what this signifies, yet draws not back a step for that; rather does he ask the King, who was beside him at the right, what this can be. The King speaks and explains to him: "Friend," he says, "do you know the meaning of this thing that you see here? You must be in great terror of it, if you care at all for your own body; for this single stake which stands apart, where you see this horn hung up, has been waiting a very long time, but we know not for whom, whether for you or someone else. Take care lest thy head be set up there; for such is the purpose of the stake. I had warned you well of that before you came here. I do not expect that you will escape hence, but that you will be killed and rent apart. For this much we know, that the stake awaits your head. And if it turns out that it be placed there, as the matter stands agreed, as soon as thy head is fixed upon it another stake will be set up beside it which will await the arrival of some one else—I know not when or whom. I will tell you nothing of the horn; but never has any one been able to blow it. However, he who shall succeed in blowing it his fame and honour will grow until it distance all those of his country, and he shall find such renown that all will come to do him honour, and will hold him to be the best of them all. Now there is no more of this matter. Have your men withdraw; for 'the Joy' will soon arrive, and will make you sorry, I suspect."

Meanwhile King Evrain leaves his side, and Erec stoops over before Enide, whose heart was in great distress, although she held her peace; for grief on lips is of no account unless it also touch the heart. And he who well knew her heart, said to her: "Fair sister dear, gentle, loyal, and prudent lady, I am acquainted with your thoughts. You are in fear, I see that well, and yet you do not know for what; but there is no reason for your dismay until you shall see that my shield is shattered and that my body is wounded, and until you see the meshes of my bright hauberk covered with blood, and my helmet broken and smashed, and me defeated and weary, so that I can no longer defend myself, but must beg and sue for mercy against my will; then you may lament, but now you have begun too soon. Gentle lady, as yet you know not what this is to be; no more do I. You are troubled without cause. But know this truly: if there were in me only so much courage as your love inspires, truly I should not fear to face any man alive. But I am foolish to vaunt myself; yet I say it not from any pride, but because I wish to comfort you. So comfort yourself, and let it be! I cannot longer tarry here, nor can you go along with me; for, as the King has ordered, I must not take you beyond this point." Then he kisses her and commends her to God, and she him. But she is much chagrined that she cannot follow and escort him, until she may learn and see what this adventure is to be, and how he will conduct himself. But since she must stay behind and cannot follow him, she remains sorrowful and grieving. And he went off alone down a path, without companion of any sort, until he came to a silver couch with a cover of gold-embroidered cloth, beneath the shade of a sycamore; and on the bed a maiden of comely body and lovely face, completely endowed with all beauty, was seated all alone. I intended to say no more of her; but whoever could consider well all her attire and her beauty might well say that never did Lavinia of Laurentum, who was so fair and comely, possess the quarter of her beauty. Erec draws near to her, wishing to see her more closely, and the onlookers go and sit down under the trees in the orchard. Then behold, there comes a knight armed with vermilion arms, and he was wondrous tall; and if he were not so immeasurably tall, under the heavens there would be none fairer than he; but, as every one averred, he was

a foot taller than any knight he knew. Before Erec caught sight of him, he
cried out: "Vassal, vassal! You are mad, upon my life, thus to approach my
damsel. I should say you are not worthy to draw near her. You will pay dearly
for your presumption, by my head! Stand back!" And Erec stops and looks at
him, and the other, too, stood still. Neither made advance until Erec had
replied all that he wished to say to him. "Friend," he says, "one can speak folly
as well as good sense. Threaten as much as you please, and I will keep silence;
for in threatening there is no sense. Do you know why? A man sometimes
thinks he has won the game who afterward loses it. So he is manifestly a fool
who is too presumptuous and who threatens too much. If there are some who
flee there are plenty who chase, but I do not fear you so much that I am going
to run away yet. I am ready to make such defence, if there is any who wishes
to offer me battle, that he will have to do his uttermost, or otherwise he
cannot escape." "Nay," quoth he, "so help me God! know that you shall have
the battle, for I defy and challenge you." And you may know, upon my word,
that then the reins were not held in. The lances they had were not light, but
were big and square; nor were they planed smooth, but were rough and
strong. Upon the shields with mighty strength they smote each other with
their sharp weapons, so that a fathom of each lance passes through the
gleaming shields. But neither touches the other's flesh, nor was either lance
cracked; each one, as quickly as he could, draws back his lance, and both
rushing together, return to the fray. One against the other rides, and so
fiercely they smite each other that both lances break and the horses fall
beneath them. But they, being seated on their steeds, sustain no harm; so they
quickly rise, for they were strong and lithe. They stand on foot in the middle
of the garden, and straightway attack each other with their green swords of
German steel, and deal great wicked blows upon their bright and gleaming
helmets, so that they hew them into bits, and their eyes shoot out flame. No
greater efforts can be made than those they make in striving and toiling to
injure and wound each other. Both fiercely smite with the gilded pommel and
the cutting edge. Such havoc did they inflict upon each other's teeth, cheeks,
nose, hands, arms, and the rest, upon temples, neck, and throat that their
bones all ache. They are very sore and very tired; yet they do not desist, but
rather only strive the more. Sweat, and the blood which flows down with it,
dim their eyes, so that they can hardly see a thing; and very often they missed
their blows, like men who did not see to wield their swords upon each other.
They can scarcely harm each other now; yet, they do not desist at all from
exercising all their strength. Because their eyes are so blinded that they
completely lose their sight, they let their shields fall to the ground, and seize

each other angrily. Each pulls and drags the other, so that they fall upon their knees. Thus, long they fight until the hour of noon is past, and the big knight is so exhausted that his breath quite fails him. Erec has him at his mercy, and pulls and drags so that he breaks all the lacing of his helmet, and forces him over at his feet. He falls over upon his face against Erec's breast, and has not strength to rise again. Though it distresses him, he has to say and own: "I cannot deny it, you have beaten me; but much it goes against my will. And yet you may be of such degree and fame that only credit will redound to me; and insistently I would request, if it may be in any way, that I might know your name, and he thereby somewhat comforted. If a better man has defeated me, I shall be glad, I promise you; but if it has so fallen out that a baser man than I has worsted me, then I must feel great grief indeed." "Friend, dost thou wish to know my name?" says Erec; "Well, I shall tell thee ere I leave here; but it will be upon condition that thou tell me now why thou art in this garden. Concerning that I will know all what is thy name and what the Joy; for I am very anxious to hear the truth from beginning to end of it." "Sire," says he, "fearlessly I will tell you all you wish to know." Erec no more withholds his name, but says: "Didst thou ever hear of King Lac and of his son Erec?" "Yea, sire, I knew him well; for I was at his father's court for many a day before I was knighted, and, if he had had his will, I should never have left him for anything." "Then thou oughtest to know me well, if thou weft ever with me at the court of my father, the King." "Then, upon my faith, it has turned out well. Now hear who has detained me so long in this garden. I will tell the truth in accordance with your injunction, whatever it may cost me. That damsel who yonder sits, loved me from childhood and I loved her. It pleased us both, and our love grew and increased, until she asked a boon of me, but did not tell me what it was. Who would deny his mistress aught? There is no lover but would surely do all his sweet-heart's pleasure without default or guile, whenever he can in any way. I agreed to her desire; but when I had agreed, she would have it, too, that I should swear. I would have done more than that for her, but she took me at my word. I made her a promise, without knowing what. Time passed until I was made a knight. King Evrain, whose nephew I am, dubbed me a knight in the presence of many honourable men in this very garden where we are. My lady, who is sitting there, at once recalled to me my word, and said that I had promised her that I would never go forth from here until there should come some knight who should conquer me by trial of arms. It was right that I should remain, for rather than break my word, I should never have pledged it. Since I knew the good there was in her, I could nor reveal or show to the one whom I hold most dear that in all this

I was displeased; for if she had noticed it, she would have withdrawn her heart, and I would not have had it so for anything that might happen. Thus my lady thought to detain me here for a long stay; she did not think that there would ever enter this garden any vassal who could conquer me. In this way she intended to keep me absolutely shut up with her all the days of my life. And I should have committed an offence if I had had resort to guile and not defeated all those against whom I could prevail; such escape would have been a shame. And I dare to assure you that I have no friend so dear that I would have feigned at all in fighting with him. Never did I weary of arms, nor did I ever refuse to fight. You have surely seen the helmets of those whom I have defeated and put to death; but the guilt of it is not mine, when one considers it aright. I could not help myself, unless I were willing to be false and recreant and disloyal. Now I have told you the truth, and be assured that it is no small honour which you have gained. You have given great joy to the court of my uncle and my friends; for now I shall be released from here; and because all those who are at the court will have joy of it, therefore those who awaited the joy called it 'Joy of the Court'. They have awaited it so long that now it will be granted them by you who have won it by your fight. You have defeated and bewitched my prowess and my chivalry. Now it is right that I tell you my name, if you would know it. I am called Mabonagrain; but I am not remembered by that name in any land where I have been, save only in this region; for never, when I was a squire, did I tell or make known my name. Sire, you knew the truth concerning all that you asked me. But I must still tell you that there is in this garden a horn which I doubt not you have seen. I cannot issue forth from here until you have blown the horn; but then you will have released me, and then the Joy will begin. Whoever shall hear and give it heed no hindrance will detain him, when he shall hear the sound of the horn, from coming straight-way to the court. Rise up, sire! Go quickly now! Go take the horn right joyfully; for you have no further cause to wait; so do that which you must do." Now Erec rose, and the other rises with him, and both approach the horn. Erec takes it and blows it, putting into it all his strength, so that the sound of it reaches far. Greatly did Enide rejoice when she heard the note, and Guivret was greatly delighted too. The King is glad, and so are his people; there is not one who is not well suited and pleased at this. No one ceases or leaves off from making merry and from song. Erec could boast that day, for never was such rejoicing made; it could not be described or related by mouth of man, but I will tell you the sum of it briefly and with few words. The news spreads through the country that thus the affair has turned out. Then there was no holding back from coming to the court. All the people hasten thither in confusion, some on foot and some on horse, without waiting for each other. And those who were in the garden hastened to remove Erec's arms, and in emulation they all sang a song about the Joy; and the ladies made up a lay which they called 'the Lay of Joy', but the lay is not well known. Erec was well sated with joy and well served to his heart's desire; but she who sat on the silver couch was not a bit pleased. The joy which she saw was not at all to her taste. But many people have to keep still and look on at what gives them pain. Enide acted graciously; because she saw her sitting pensive, alone on the couch, she felt moved to go and speak with her and tell her about her affairs and about herself, and to strive, if possible, to make her tell in return about herself, if it did not cause her too great distress. Enide thought to go alone, wishing to take no one with her, but some of the most noble and fairest dames and damsels followed her out of affection to bear her company, and also to comfort her to whom the joy brings great chagrin; for she assumed that now her lover would be no longer with her so much as he had been, inasmuch as he desired to leave the garden. However disappointing it may be, no one can prevent his going away, for the hour and the time have come. Therefore the tears ran down her face from her eyes. Much more than I can say was she grieving and distressed; nevertheless she sat up straight. But she does not care so much for any of those who try to comfort her that she ceases her moan. Enide salutes her kindly; but for a while the other could not reply a word, being prevented by the sighs and sobs which torment and distress her. Some time it was before the damsel returned her salutation, and when she had looked at her and examined her for a while, it seemed that she had seen and known her before. But not being very certain of it, she was not slow to inquire from whence she was, of what country, and where her lord was born; she inquires who they both are. Enide replies briefly and tells her the truth, saying: "I am the niece of the Count who holds sway over Lalut, the daughter of his own sister; at Lalut I was born and brought up." The other cannot help smiling, without hearing more, for she is so delighted that she forgets her sorrow. Her heart leaps with joy which she cannot conceal. She runs and embraces Enide, saying: "I am your cousin! This is the very truth, and you are my father's niece; for he and your father are brothers. But I suspect that you do not know and have never heard how I came into this country. The Count, your uncle, was at war, and to him there came to fight for pay knights of many lands. Thus, fair cousin, it came about, that with these hireling knights there came one who was the nephew of the king of Brandigan. He was with my father almost a year. That was, I think, twelve years ago, and I was still but a little child. He was very handsome and attractive. There we had an understanding between us that pleased us both. I never had any wish but his, until at last he began to love me and promised and swore to me that he would always be my lover, and that he would bring me here; that pleased us both alike. He could not wait, and I was longing to come hither with him; so we both came away, and no one knew of it but ourselves. In those days you and I were both young and little girls. I have told you the truth; so now tell me in turn, as I have told you, all about your lover, and by what adventure he won you." "Fair cousin, he married me in such a way that my father knew all about it, and my mother was greatly pleased. All our relatives knew it and rejoiced over it, as they should do. Even the Count was glad. For he is so good a knight that better cannot be found, and he does not need to prove his honour and knighthood, and he is of very gentle birth: I do not think that any can be his equal. He loves me much, and I love him more, and our love cannot be greater. Never yet could I withhold my love from him, nor should I do so. For is not my lord the son of a king? For did he not take me when I was poor and naked? Through him has such honour come to me that never was any such vouchsafed to a poor helpless girl. And if it please you, I will tell you without lying how I came to be thus raised up; for never will I be slow to tell the story." Then she told and related to her how Erec came to Lalut; for she had no desire to conceal it. She told her the adventure word for word, without omission. But I pass over it now, because he who tells a story twice makes his tale now tiresome. While they were thus conversing, one lady slipped away alone, who sent and told it all to the gentlemen, in order to increase and heighten their pleasure too. All those who heard it rejoiced at this news. And when Mabonagrain knew it he was delighted for his sweetheart because now she was comforted. And she who bore them quickly the news made them all happy in a short space. Even the King was glad for it; although he was very happy before, yet now he is still happier, and shows Erec great honour. Enide leads away her fair cousin, fairer than Helen, more graceful and charming. Now Erec and Mabonagrain, Guivret and King Evrain, and all the others run to meet them and salute them and do them honour, for no one is grudging or holds back. Mabonagrain makes much of Enide, and she of him. Erec and Guivret, for their part, rejoice over the damsel as they all kiss and embrace each other. They propose to return to the castle, for they have stayed too long in the garden. They are all prepared to go out; so they sally forth joyfully, kissing each other on the way. All go out after the King, but before they reached the castle, the nobles were assembled from all the country around, and all those who knew of the Joy, and who could do so, came hither. Great was the gathering and the press.

Every one, high and low, rich and poor, strives to see Erec. Each thrusts himself before the other, and they all salute him and bow before him, saying constantly: "May God save him through whom joy and gladness come to our court! God save the most blessed man whom God has ever brought into being!" Thus they bring him to the court, and strive to show their glee as their hearts dictate. Breton zithers, harps, and viols sound, fiddles, psalteries, and other stringed instruments, and all kinds of music that one could name or mention. But I wish to conclude the matter briefly without too long delay. The King honours him to the extent of his power, as do all the others ungrudgingly. There is no one who does not gladly offer to do his service. Three whole days the Joy lasted, before Erec could get away. On the fourth he would no longer tarry for any reason they could urge. There was a great crowd to accompany him and a very great press when it came to taking leave. If he had wished to reply to each one, he would not have been able in half a day to return the salutations individually. The nobles he salutes and embraces; the others he commends to God in a word, and salutes them. Enide, for her part, is not silent when she takes leave of the nobles. She salutes them all by name, and they in turn do the like. Before she goes, she kisses her cousin very tenderly and embraces her. Then they go and the Joy is over.

They go off and the others return. Erec and Guivret do not tarry, but keep joyfully on their way, until they came in nine days to Robais, where they were told the King was. The day before he had been bled privately in his apartments; with him he had only five hundred nobles of his household. Never before at any time was the King found so alone, and he was much distressed that he had no more numerous suite at his court. At that time a messenger comes running, whom they had sent ahead to apprise the King of their approach. This man came in before the assembly, found the King and all his people, and saluting him correctly, said: "I am a messenger of Erec and of Guivret the Little." Then he told him how they were coming to see him at his court. The King replies: "Let them be welcome, as valiant and gallant gentlemen! Nowhere do I know of any better than they two. By their presence my court will be much enhanced." Then he sent for the Queen and told her the news. The others have their horses saddled to go and meet the gentlemen. In such haste are they to mount that they did not put on their spurs. I ought to state briefly that the crowd of common people, including squires, cooks, and butlers, had already entered the town to prepare for the lodgings. The main party came after, and had already drawn so near that they had entered the town. Now the two parties have met each other, and salute and kiss each other. They come to the lodgings and make themselves comfortable, removing their hose and making their toilet by donning their rich robes. When they were completely decked out, they took their way to the court. They come to court, where the King sees them, and the Queen, who is beside herself with impatience to see Erec and Enide. The King makes them take seats beside him, kisses Erec and Guivret; about Enide's neck he throws his arms and kisses her repeatedly, in his great joy. Nor is the Queen slow in embracing Erec and Enide. One might well rejoice to see her now so full of joy. Every one enters with spirit into the merry-making. Then the King causes silence to be made, and appeals to Erec and asks news of his adventures. When the noise had ceased, Erec began his story, telling him of his adventures, without forgetting any detail. Do you think now that I shall tell you what motive he had had in starting out? Nay, for you know the whole truth about this and the rest, as I have revealed it to you. To tell the story again would burden me; for the tale is not short, that any one should wish to begin it afresh and re-embelish it, as he told and related it: of the three knights whom he defeated, and then of the five, and then of the Count who strove to do him harm, and then of the two giants—all in order, one after the other, he told him of his adventures up to the point where he met Count Oringle of Limors. "Many a danger have you gone through, fair gentle friend," said the King to him; "now tarry in this country at my court, as you are wont to do." "Sire, since you wish it, I shall remain very gladly three or four years entire. But ask Guivret to remain here too a request in which I would fain join." The King prays him to remain, and he consents to stay. So they both stay: the King kept them with him, and held them dear and honoured them.

Erec stayed at court, together with Guivret and Enide, until the death of his father, the king, who was an old man and full of years. The messengers then started out: the nobles who went to seek him, and who were the greatest men of the land, sought and searched for him until they found him at Tintagel three weeks before Christmas; they told him the truth what had happened to his old, white-haired father, and how he now was dead and gone. This grieved Erec much more than he showed before the people. But sorrow is not seemly in a king, nor does it become a king to mourn. There at Tintagel where he was, he caused vigils for the dead and Masses to be sung; he promised and kept his promises, as he had vowed to the religious houses and churches; he did well all that he ought to do: he chose out more than one hundred and sixty-nine of the wretched poor, and clothed them all in new garments. To the poor clerks and priors he gave, as was right, black copes and warm linings to wear beneath. For God's sake he did great good to all: to those who were in need he distributed more than a barrel of small coins. When he had shared his wealth, he then did a very wise thing in receiving his land from the King's hand; and then he begged the King to crown him at his court. The King bade him quickly be prepared; for they shall both be crowned, he together with his wife, at the approaching Christmastide; and he added: "You must go hence to Nantes in Brittany; there you shall carry a royal ensign with crown on head and sceptre in hand; this gift and privilege I bestow upon you." Erec thanked the King, and said that that was a noble gift. At Christmas the King assembles all his nobles, summoning them individually and commanding them to come to Nantes. He summoned them all, and none stayed behind. Erec, too, sent word to many of his followers, and summoned them to come thither; but more came than he had bidden, to serve him and do him honour. I cannot tell you or relate who each one was, and what his name; but whoever came or did not come, the father and mother of my lady Enide were not forgotten. Her father was sent for first of all, and he came to court in handsome style, like a great lord and a chatelain. There was no great crowd of chaplains or of silly, gaping yokels, but of excellent knights and of people well equipped. Each day they made a long day's journey, and rode on each day with great joy and great display, until on Christmas eve they came to the city of Nantes. They made no halt until they entered the great hall where the King and his courtiers were. Erec and Enide see them, and you may know how glad they were. To meet them they quickly make their way, and salute and embrace them, speaking to them tenderly and showing their delight as they should. When they had rejoiced together, taking each other by the hand, they all four came before the King, saluting him and likewise the Queen, who was sitting by his side. Taking his host by the hand, Erec said: "Sire, behold my good host, my kind friend, who did me such honour that he made me master in his own house. Before he knew anything about me, he lodged me well and handsomely. All that he had he made over to me, and even his daughter he bestowed upon me, without the advice or counsel of any one." "And this lady with him," the King inquires, "who is she?" Erec does not conceal the truth: "Sire," says he, "of this lady I may say that she is the mother of my wife." "Is she her mother?" "Yes, truly, sire." "Certainly, I may then well say that fair and comely should be the flower born of so fair a stem, and better the fruit one picks; for sweet is the smell of what springs from good. Fair is Enide and fair she should be in all reason and by right; for her mother is a very handsome lady, and her father is a goodly knight. Nor does she in aught belie them; for she descends and inherits directly from them both in many respects." Then the King ceases and sits down, bidding them be seated too. They do not disobey his command, but straightway take seats. Now is Enide filled with joy when she sees her father and mother, for a very long time had passed since she had seen them. Her happiness now is greatly increased, for she was delighted and happy, and she showed it all she could, but she could not make such demonstration but that her joy was yet greater. But I wish to say no more of that, for my heart draws me toward the court which was now assembled in force. From many a different country there were counts and dukes and kings, Normans, Bretons. Scotch, and Irish: from England and Cornwall there was a very rich gathering of nobles; for from Wales to Anjou, in Maine and in Poitou, there was no knight of importance, nor lady of quality, but the best and the most elegant were at the court at Nantes, as the King had bidden them. Now hear, if you will, the great joy and grandeur, the display and the wealth, that was exhibited at the court. Before the hour of nones had sounded, King Arthur dubbed four hundred knights or more all sons of counts and of kings. To each one he gave three horses and two pairs of suits, in order that his court may make a better showing. Puissant and lavish was the King; for the mantles he bestowed were not of serge, nor of rabbit-skins, nor of cheap brown fur, but of heavy silk and ermine, of spotted fur and flowered silks, bordered with heavy and stiff gold braid. Alexander, who conquered so much that he subdued the whole world, and who was so lavish and rich, compared with him was poor and mean. Caesar, the Emperor of Rome, and all the kings whose names you hear in stories and in epic songs, did not distribute at any feast so much as Arthur gave on the day that he crowned Erec; nor would Caesar and Alexander dare to spend so much as he spent at the court. The raiment was taken from the chests and spread about freely through the halls; one could take what he would, without restraint. In the midst of the court, upon a rug, stood thirty bushels of bright sterlings; for since the time of Merlin until that day sterlings had currency throughout Britain. There all helped themselves, each one carrying away that night all that he wanted to his lodging-place. At nine o'clock on Christmas day, all came together again at court. The great joy that is drawing near for him had completely filched Erec's heart away. The tongue and the mouth of no man, however skilful, could describe the third, or the fourth, or the fifth part of the display which marked his coronation. So it is a mad enterprise I undertake in wishing to attempt to describe it. But since I must make the effort, come what may, I shall not fail to relate a part of it, as best I may.

The King had two thrones of white ivory, well constructed and new, of one pattern and style. He who made them beyond a doubt was a very skilled and cunning craftsman. For so precisely did he make the two alike in height, in breadth, and in ornamentation, that you could nor look at them from every side to distinguish one from the other and find in one aught that was not in the other. There was no part of wood, but all of gold and fine ivory. Well were they carved with great skill, for the two corresponding sides of each bore the representation of a leopard, and the other two a dragon's shape. A knight named Bruiant of the Isles had made a gift and present of them to King Arthur and the Queen. King Arthur sat upon the one, and upon the other he made Erec sit, who was robed in watered silk. As we read in the story, we find the description of the robe, and in order that no one may say that I lie, I quote as my authority Macrobius, who devoted himself to the description of it. Macrobius instructs me how to describe, according as I have found it in the book, the workmanship and the figures of the cloth. Four fairies had made it with great skill and mastery. One represented there geometry, how it estimates and measures the extent of the heavens and the earth, so that nothing is lacking there; and then the depth and the height, and the width, and the length; then it estimates, besides, how broad and deep the sea is, and thus measures the whole world. Such was the work of the first fairy. And the second devoted her effort to the portrayal of arithmetic, and she strove hard to represent clearly how it wisely enumerates the days and the hours of time, and the water of the sea drop by drop, and then all the sand, and the stars one by one, knowing well how to tell the truth, and how many leaves there are in the woods: such is the skill of arithmetic that numbers have never deceived her, nor will she ever be in error when she wishes to apply her sense to them. The third design was that of music, with which all merriment finds itself in accord, songs and harmonies, and sounds of string: of harp, of Breton violin, and of viol. This piece of work was good and fine; for upon it were portrayed all the instruments and all the pastimes. The fourth, who next performed her task, executed a most excellent work; for the best of the arts she there portrayed. She undertook astronomy, which accomplishes so many marvels and draws inspiration from the stars, the moon, and the sun. Nowhere else does it seek counsel concerning aught which it has to do. They give it good and sure advice. Concerning whatever inquiry it make of them, whether in the past or in the future, they give it information without falsehood and without deception. This work was portrayed on the stuff of which Erec's robe was made, all worked and woven with thread of gold. The fur lining that was sewed within, belonged to some strange beasts whose heads are all white, and whose necks are as black as mulberries, and which have red backs and green bellies, and dark blue tail. These beasts live in India and they are called "barbiolets". They eat nothing but spices, cinnamon, and fresh cloves. What shall I tell you of the mantle? It was very rich and fine and handsome; it had four stones in the tassels—two chrysolites on one side, and two amethysts on the other, which were mounted in gold.

As yet Enide had not come to the palace. When the King sees that she delays, he bids Gawain go quickly to bring her and the Queen. Gawain hastens and was not slow, and with him King Cadoalant and the generous King of Galloway. Guivret the Little accompanies them, followed by Yder the son of Nut. So many of the other nobles ran thither to escort the two ladies that they would have sufficed to overcome a host; for there were more than a thousand of them. The Queen had made her best effort to adorn Enide. Into the palace they brought her the courteous Gawain escorting her on one side, and on the other the generous King of Galloway, who loved her dearly on account of Erec who was his nephew. When they came to the palace, King Arthur came quickly toward them, and courteously seated Enide beside Erec; for he wished to do her great honour. Now he orders to be brought forth from his treasure two massive crowns of fine gold. As soon as he had spoken and given the command, without delay the crowns were brought before him, all sparkling with carbuncles, of which there were four in each. The light of the moon is nothing compared with the light which the least of the carbuncles could shed. Because of the radiance which they shed, all those who were in the palace were so dazzled that for a moment they could see nothing; and even the King was amazed, and yet filled with satisfaction, when he saw them to be so clear and bright. He had one of them held by two damsels, and the other by two gentlemen. Then he bade the bishops and priors and the abbots of the Church step forward and anoint the new King, as the Christian practice is. Now all the prelates, young and old, came forward; for at the court there were a great number of bishops and abbots. The Bishop of Nantes himself, who was a very worthy and saintly man, anointed the new King in a very holy and becoming manner, and placed the crown upon his head. King Arthur had a sceptre brought which was very fine. Listen to the description of the sceptre, which was clearer than a pane of glass, all of one solid emerald, fully as large as your fist. I dare to tell you in very truth that in all the world there is no manner of fish, or of wild behest, or of man, or of flying bird that was not worked and chiselled upon it with its proper figure. The sceptre was handed to the King, who looked at it with amazement; then he put it without delay into King Erec's right hand; and now he was King as he ought to be. Then he crowned Enide in turn. Now the bells ring for Mass, and they go to the main church to hear the Mass and service; they go to pray at the cathedral. You would have seen weeping with joy the father of Queen Enide and her mother, Carsenefide. In truth this was her mother's name, and her father's name was Liconal. Very happy were they both. When they came to the cathedral, the procession came out from the church with relics and treasures to meet them. Crosses and prayerbooks and censers and reliquaries, with all the holy relics, of which there were many in the church, were all brought out to meet them; nor was there any lack of chants made. Never were seen so many kings, counts, dukes, and nobles together at a Mass, and the press was so great and thick that the church was completely filled. No low-born man could enter there, but only ladies and knights. Outside the door of the church a great number still remained, so many were there come together who could not get inside the church. When they had heard all the Mass they returned to the palace. It was all prepared and decorated: tables set and cloths spread five hundred tables and more were there; but I do not wish to make you believe a thing which does not seem true. It would seem too great a lie were I to say that five hundred tables were set in rows in one palace, so I will not say it; rather were there five hails so filled with them that with great difficulty could one make his way among the tables. At each table there was in truth a king or a duke or a count; and full a hundred knights were seated at each table. A thousand knights served the bread, and a thousand served the wine, and a thousand the meat—all of them dressed in fresh fur robes of ermine. All are served with divers dishes. Even if I did not see them, I might still be able to tell you about them; but I must attend to something else than to tell you what they had to eat. They had enough, without wanting more; joyfully and liberally they were served to their heart's desire.

When this celebration was concluded, the King dismissed the assemblage of kings, dukes, and counts, of which the number was immense, and of the other humble folk who had come to the festival. He rewarded them liberally with horses, arms and silver, cloths and brocades of many kinds, because of his generosity, and because of Erec whom he loved so much. Here the story ends at last.

CPSIA information can be obtained at www.ICGtesting.com
Printed in the USA
LVOW08s2001080614

389099LV00001B/186/P